MW00916568

Praise for **The Rest of Your Life**

"In a world where money has replaced morals, lies have replaced truth, billionaire shave replaced public servants, sycophancy has replaced principle, corporations have replaced community, and technology has replaced simple human interaction,what are we to do? How are we to adapt and thrive, while still remaining true to ourselves? In this engaging collection of stories – covering human relationships strained by political division, Matrix-esque mind-control,page-turning political brinksmanship, and much more – Chris Kremidas-Courtney holds up a mirror to our individual and collective trauma in a world that's changing too fast, and reminds us that the choices we make today will, in infinite ways, determine how 'the rest of our lives' unfurl."

- Michael M. Bowden, attorney and journalist; author, *The Goddess and the Guru* and *Gifts from the Goddess*

"Fasten your seat belts for science fiction with a twist. Each of these compelling stories could happen in the future... and some of them sooner than we think."

- Alice Stollmeyer, Executive Director at Defend Democracy

"Thoughtful, prescient and impactful."

- Miko Matsumura, Managing partner at Gumi Cryptos Capital

"Compelling tales that offer profound insights into a future we must prepare for...a must-read for anyone interested in the intersection of technology and global affairs."

- Hanna Linderstål, CEO of Earhart Business Protection Agency

"A gripping and thought-provoking political thriller that master-fully weaves personal integrity, geopolitical tension, and speculative technology into a narrative as engaging as it is timely. This book is a must-read for anyone fascinated by the intersections of power, moral-ity, and the uncertain future of global alliances."
  - Thanos Sitistas, Founder and Director of Greece Fact Check

"These stories bring potential futures to life in a creative, under-standable and relatable way."
  - Miriam Fugfugosh, Global Executive Educator

"Tom Clancy meets John Grisham meets Alex Toffler and George Orwell. We need to get ready for the rest of our lives. Chris Kremi-das-Courney's latest book provides needed glimpses into the not too distant future -- and in fact, the current "now" that many of us need help comprehending. These five prescient short stories are rich with relatable characters, riveting dialogue, and scenarios that offer deft insights into the looming near future. They are also mirrors we'd do well to gaze upon- even as such gazing may cause us to gasp and wince with the sober recognition of what we've collectively allowed and are complicit in. Buckle-up folks,there's turbulence ahead."
  - Roger Wolsey, author, *Kissing Fish: Christianity for People Who Don't Like Christianity;* and *Discovering Fire: Spiritual Practices That Transform Lives.*

# THE REST OF YOUR LIFE

## FIVE STORIES OF YOUR FUTURE

CHRIS KREMIDAS-COURTNEY

BRAHMALOKA PRESS

Copyright © 2024 by Chris Kremidas-Courtney

All rights reserved.

ISBN: 9798343826036 (Hardcover)  ISBN: 9798344579658 (Paperback)

No part of this publication may be reproduced, distributed, or transmitted in any form or by any means, including photocopying, recording, or other electronic or mechanical methods, without the prior written permission of the publisher, except as permitted by U.S. copyright law. For permission requests, contact [include publisher/author contact info].

The story, all names, characters, and incidents portrayed in this production are fictitious. No identification with actual persons (living or deceased), places, buildings, countries, universities, companies, and products is intended or should be inferred.

Book Cover by Author  Cover Photograph by Dean Fikar (Under License via Shutterstock)

First edition 2024

# CONTENTS

For Maya Georg, my everything

This is a work of fiction. Names, characters, businesses, countries, places, schools, universities, events and incidents are either the products of the author's imagination or used in a fictitious manner. Any resemblance to actual persons, living or dead, or actual events is purely coincidental.

# FOREWORD

As I write this, Donald Trump has won the White House. Silicon Valley's tech billionaires have already been signalling they want to work with the incoming administration to accelerate imagined futures of outer space (satellite Internet, asteroid mining, Mars exploration),inner space (artificial neural networks, brain-computer interfaces), and cyberspace (Metaverses, VR, Augmented Reality). The rest of us get to live in a world of algorithmic surveillance, radicalized and polarized political discourse, skyrocketing inequality, and geopolitical and environmental breakdown.

Chris Kremidas-Courtney's *The Rest of Your Life* uses speculative fiction as it should be used, to hold a mirror up to the world we live in now. Chris—a seasoned policy specialist in global security and future threats—draws on decades of experience to craft a collection of engaging, grounded, techno-dystopian narratives that show why we should care much more about the imagined futures of the world's wealthiest individuals.

With a career spanning the US military, think-tanks, intergovernmental and transnational organizations, Chris uses fiction to interrogate the technical systems and shifting social frameworks that increasingly govern our lives. The characters in *The Rest of Your Life* inhabit futures where technologies mold and constrain them in ways that feel unnervingly possible. The collection examines themes of control, personal freedom, and the dynamics of technological power beneath the surface of daily life.

A central tension throughout is the question of individual agency versus systemic control. We meet characters caught in the grips of corporate surveillance infrastructures, trapped by algorithms and economic pressures that gradually erode their personal freedoms. Each story shows the psychological effects on individuals living in a highly complex, information-dense world—a perspective shaped by Chris's background in NATO and global defense circles.

There is hope, too. Through this work of fiction, Chris invites us not just to imagine the consequences of our present trajectories but to consider how we might steer toward different paths. *The Rest of Your Life* is a journey through potential futures that feels plausible and deeply consequential, offering both a warning and a call to action.

As Dennis Gabor put it: "the future cannot be predicted, but futures can be invented". Chris Kremidas-Courtney challenges us to shape these futures consciously, to craft a world worth inhabiting. This collection is therefore both a mirror and a map through the looking glass—a sober invitation to confront the world of imagined futures before they become the world where we live the rest of our lives.

**Joe Litobarski,**
*Maastricht, 8 November 2024*

# CHAPTER ONE

# A DREAM YEAR

Riding your bike you need to be alert, especially on a night like this. Holly remembered the advice of her friend Mike, an avid cyclist. He said to "ride as if you are invisible and assume they don't see you." This advice made her commutes to and from her job at Northern Arizona University much safer and saved her life at least twice in the past year.

A light rain started to fall as she got a few blocks from her house. If it was still April, snow would be falling but it was mid-May it was just a chilly rain.

She pulled up in the driveway and saw the lights were on so her roommate Megan must have been home. Opening the door and pulling the bike through was always awkward. She needed to do it quickly while also making sure Megan's cat did not run out into the night.

This time she only partly succeeded. She kept the cat inside. But her bike fell against a small table by the door. This sent a tray of keys and change flying. It did not help that she did not see the Amazon box at the door that she tripped over while coming in.

"Welcome home klutz!" said Megan from the living room sofa.

Holly sheepishly replied "hey, sorry" as she hung up her damp jacket. Then, she started picking things up from the floor and putting them back on the entry table.

"There's a box here for you" Holly said and handed it to Megan, who set it aside and kept watching the TV.

"You hungry?" Holly asked. Megan smiled and nodded her head then went back to watching TV. Holly went into the kitchen and started to cook mushrooms and arborio rice. Their living arrangement seemed easier since both Holly and Megan were vegetarians.

A while later, Holly put down two big bowls on the coffee table. They began to eat and catch up on their days. Megan launched into a rant about her boss at the tech startup she worked for and how he never seemed to listen. She worked remotely, so at least she seldom needed to see her boss face-to-face. But once she started describing the coding she wanted to use to improve the software, Holly held a hand up.

"Whoa, I've no idea what you are talking about" Holly said.

Holly often had to stop and ask Megan, the tech nerd, to explain what she was talking about it went over her head.

"OK yoga dork," laughed Megan.

Holly made a funny face and started to lift one foot as if to place it behind her head.

"Ooh, not warmed up yet. Maybe tomorrow morning." Holly said as she lowered her leg back down.

"Shhh, Rachel Maddow is on now!" Megan said, and both watched intently.

"Oh gawd, this guy again?" Holly remarked as the program delved into the politics of Charles Pelley. He was the leading Christian Nationalist presidential candidate whose entire platform was about putting down women, demonizing immigrants, and attacking queer people.

"He's such a tool" Megan hissed.

Later as Megan took the bowls back into the kitchen, Holly called out.

"What's in the box?"

Megan put the bowls into the sink and started to rinse them. Over the sound of rushing water, she said "I think it's my new pillow."

"Who gets a pillow from Amazon?" Holly asked.

"Oh, it's not just any pillow" Megan replied.

A few minutes later, Megan came back to the living room and opened the box to reveal her new brainwave pillow.

"I can't wait to try this! I hope it gets me over all that insomnia" Megan said.

"I thought you were just a night owl" Holly replied then asked, "how does it work?"

"It's a smart pillow. It uses neurotechnology to sense your brain waves. Then, it sends the right signal to your brain to help you sleep," Megan answered.

"Oh wow! Well, you do always have the latest of everything" Holly observed "I hope it helps."

"I'm gonna sleep like a baby tonight!" Megan grinned and went to bed early. Holly stayed up late working on a painting she had been wanting to finish for weeks.

Late Saturday morning they always rode their bikes to meet a few friends for coffee at Macy's near the NAU campus. The sun was out so they all sat out on the tables out front. Today they were joined by Cassandra, a PhD forestry student from Santa Fe and a local couple, Kelly and Tessie, who ran a shop that sells musical instruments, spiritual ornaments, and such.

Once they all sat down, Cassandra started the conversation.

"So, there's a new band at Flag Brew tonight, wanna go?"

"Ugh, not me. After this I am going back to take a nap then work on my painting all weekend. I stayed up late working on it last night and it's really coming together." Holly replied.

"I'm down!" Megan happily replied. "Unlike my roomie, I slept great last night."

"So that thing worked, eh?" Holly asked.

"What thing?" Tessie inquired.

"An electric device?" Kelly asked impishly.

Megan smirked and responded, "no silly, an electronic device."

"Ooh" everyone cooed.

Megan went on, "it's a smart pillow that makes you sleep better."

"So how does your bionic pillow make you sleep better, does it give you a massage?"Kelly asked.

"It reads your brain waves and then sends signals to help you relax and sleep better." Megan said.

"That sounds more like voodoo" Holly giggled.

"Said the girl who still uses a prehistoric phone" Megan replied.

Holly made a face and responded, "It's not that old, and it's an iPhone!"

"Yeah, but it's like an iPhone from 2005" Megan quipped.

Feeling a bit smug, Holly replied "Its works and it's paid for!"

Turning back to the group, Megan said "You guys should totally try it."

Tessie replied, "Not my thing, too weird and probably expensive" and Holly chimed in with " no thanks." Kelly just made a face and shook his head.

Getting back to the subject of Saturday night plans, Cassandra asked "so who else is going to Flag Brew tonight?"

A few weeks later, while watching TV one night, Megan told Holly she was having strange dreams. The dreams involved immigrants. She was still sleeping well but wondered if it was all the campaign ads on TV that were doing it to her.

"Probably, I mean maybe we should watch less TV because those ads are everywhere, and they make me sick." Holly said.

"Yeah, me too. Plus, its summer now so we should be out having fun instead!" Megan replied.

Holly smiled and said, "Oh yeah."

They spent June going bouldering after work. It was easier now with warmer weather and longer days. Holly finished another painting and was almost ready for her opening at a downtown gallery in July. Maybe she could get lucky, and some tourists would buy up all her new pieces.

Megan's work started to slack off after finishing a big project for a Tucson customer. But, instead of doing like most people in Flagstaff and spending more time outside, she spent more time watching TV and scrolling online.

One night Holly came home and found Megan watching Fox News.

"Dude, seriously?" Holly said.

Megan, looking embarrassed replied "I just wanna see what they're saying. Besides, we can't just live in our own bubble."

Not convinced," Holly responded. "They're against our right to choose what happens with our bodies. They're against equal rights for women, people of color, and queer people. They always support the billionaires. What more is there to learn?"

Megan sheepishly replied, "I just wanna see why they are so worked up about immigration."

"It's because they are brown, we know that. Holly said. "If they were Danish, I'm sure they wouldn't care."

Feeling frustrated, Holly went into the kitchen, made some soup, and ate it in her room.

By the end of the week, Holly and Megan had put that behind them. Megan came to Holly's Friday night yoga class. Noticing Megan's increasing isolation at home, Holly was trying to pull her roommate out of the house more often.

Afterwards, they went to a friend's party. Soon, it seemed everyone started talking about the upcoming election. They had to almost shout to hear each other over the music and loud chatter in the house.

"But maybe they have a point" Megan was overheard saying to a small group in the kitchen. One of them walked out of the kitchen and brushed past Holly in the living room saying, "what the hell is with your roommate?"

Holly entered the kitchen to the sound of shouting voices, most of them aimed at Megan. She then heard Megan reply to the group. "I mean, look at all the crimes by these immigrants. We can't just ignore that."

"No!" Said Mike, still in his cycling clothes and standing by the stove. "Every study shows that immigrants commit crimes less than we do!"

Megan shrugged in response. The rest of the group shuffled out past Holly until she was alone with Megan.

Aghast, Holly blurted out "dude, whoa!"

Feeling defensive, Megan replied "oh you wanna to pick on me too?" as she crossed her arms.

"So, you support Pelley now?" Holly asked.

Letting out a long breath, Megan answered "not really, I just think we need to be more open minded."

"About what, racism?" Holly spat out.

Megan set her jaw and replied, "It isn't racism, these are real concerns."

Holly shouted, "since when do you believe Fox News?" her Queens accent becoming more pronounced.

"I don't watch them" Megan replied, "I've been doing my own research."

Holly sighed and said "OK, I want to see that research."

Megan asked, "can we just go home now?"

"OK," Holly replied. They walked out through the party, past many staring and shaking heads.

The next day, Holly woke up. She wondered how to talk to her friend and roommate about her obvious shift in political views. She thought back to how they first met three years before at a meeting during a weekend trail cleanup that autumn. Each year, tourists from around the world leave garbage along the trailheads. And every year, the locals picked it up. Well, at least some of them.

Megan and Holly got put into the same group. They spent a September day filling garbage bags with soiled diapers, beer bottles, toilet paper, plastic bottles, and more. At some point that morning, a few of them started to make up stories behind some of the more egregious trash piles, each on adding a funnier detail to the story until they were bent over laughing.

Afterwards, they all went for coffee. There, Holly and Megan kept inventing stories and laughing so much that they made a scene. Once the laughter died down, they talked about their concern that tourism was ruining their local environment which led into politics, dating, and food.

They hung out almost every week that fall. When Megan's room-mate moved out in January, she asked Holly if she wanted to move in. After that they were inseparable,and half their friends wondered if they were in a romantic relationship.

Holly pondered their relationship over her coffee that morning. She kept reminiscing about the past and wondering how she can see what was going on with her friend and to hear why she had shifted so much. Megan was a techie who loves to deal in science and facts, Holly figured it would be easy. Just show her the facts and Megan would snap out of it.

So, Holly pulled out her laptop and began searching for information on immigration. She found data on their positive impact on communities. Their crime rates were lower than citizens'. She also read a few articles about why Pelley and the far right like to blame immigrants. And, why so many people believed it.

Megan was sleeping late. So, Holly wanted to ride her bike downtown to get a smoothie and a breakfast burrito. She went to pull her bike from a rack in the hallway when she noticed the back tire was low on air. She looked around for the air pump. Then she remembered it was out in the garage, a place she avoided it always smelled rotten.

Holly went to open the door to the garage and for some reason it would not open all the way. She had to put her shoulder against it to push something out of the way that was blocking it. Once she managed to step inside, she saw the reason why.

The garage was half-filled with Sheimu boxes. Soon, they could look like the end scene from the first Indiana Jones movie. They must have been stacked 4-5 feet high and most of them were not even opened. Holly let out a long sigh and shook her head. She saw the pump on the near wall and shimmied her way between stacks of boxes to get it, then had to shimmy out the same way.

She pumped up her bike tire and left the house.

Later that afternoon Holly returned and found Megan sitting on the couch with a bowl of cereal in her hand.

"Hey" Holly said as she hung her bike and helmet on the wall.

"Hey" Megan mumbled.

"How are you feeling today?" Holly asked.

"I keep having these vivid dreams but I slept great. So, does everybody hate me now?" Megan replied.

Holly scrunched her face and said, "aw c'mon, nobody hates you."

"Even you do now" Megan said,

"Dude, don't be ridiculous. We've been through too much for me to ever hate you. OK, maybe when you leave a sink full of dirty dishes but that's it." Holly replied,trying to lighten the mood as she sat on the couch next to Megan.

Megan mumbled something unintelligible.

Holly then changed tack and asked, "how about we go down to Oak Creek Canyon and do a soak?"

Megan said nothing and kept eating her cereal.

Feeling frustrated, Holly said "OK, then can we talk about last night?"

"What about last night?" Megan said. "You mean everyone picking on me for having different ideas?"

"No, we're just not used to hearing you agreeing with Pelley and Fox News." Holly replied and motioned over to where the cat was rustling inside of a box. "And what's with all the Sheimu boxes? What's going on with you?"

Feeling defensive, Megan said "I am trying to keep an open mind. You know, maybe that last election was stolen. I mean, think about it."

Holly gasped and said, "There's no evidence that says that could even remotely be true. Jeez!"

Holly continued "I remember this friend who had so much compassion for people who are pushed to the margins of society. What happened to her?"

"Of course, I still care, but who cares about us? Aren't we the ones paying for them?" Megan retorted.

"Paying what?" Holly responded. "They work for sub-minimum wages and do all the hard dirty work no one else wants to do!"

Holly then proceeded to quote the various facts and studies she found on the positive impact of immigration, but Megan would not hear it. She showed her the numbers and studies on her laptop screen, but Megan only became more agitated and kept reciting talking points from Pelley and his followers.

Finally, Megan blurted out "why are you attacking me? This is how I feel."

Holly closed her eyes and said, "It's like I don't even know you anymore."

Then she closed her laptop, went to her room, and laid down.

The next few weeks of July passed, and they did not talk about politics. In fact, they barely spoke at all. Holly stayed active outside. Megan mostly stayed inside, watching TV and reading on her laptop. An uneasy tension filled the house. More gadgets and white elephant items arrived in Sheimu boxes. Holly even wondered if this friendship was worth saving and whether she should find a new place to live.

One day in early August after Holly finally dragged Megan out for a hike, they both sat down and turned on the TV. The announcer was talking about the impact of dream advertising. It was influencing people all over the country and making them change their minds about all sorts of things. The screen then showed a picture of various "smart pillows." It included the one that Megan bought months before.

"Oh my God Megan, that's your pillow!" Holly shouted. "That explains so much!"

Offended and defensive, Megan replied "No it doesn't, it helps me sleep but has no impact on how I think."

"Are you sure?" Holly asked. "Have you been to the garage lately?"

"Ugh" Megan whispered as she shook her head.

"And what else explains the most progressive person I know suddenly being against immigrants and becoming a hoarder?" Holly asked.

"I'm not against anyone. I just think we need to get these things under control." Megan replied.

"With detention camps and deportations? Because that is what Pelley promised to do." Holly spat out.

Megan sat in silence and would not even look at Holly. This silence between them lingered on as they barely spoke during the next two weeks. Holly feared their friendship was permanently ruptured. But now she had a much better idea of what happened to her friend that summer.

Holly read more about dream advertising and how it worked. It used smart pillows to read brain waves with a built-in EEG. Then, they sent soothing waves to help someone sleep.

The smart pillow was also connected to Wi-Fi. This allowed the device to exchange data with the company server, which helped monitor sleep trends and tweak the signals that help someone sleep. This connection also let them do product placement in someone's dreams. It was buried in the user agreement which no one reads anyway.

The more Holly read, she also learned that political action groups and campaigns were also using dream advertising. "Holy shit" she thought. "That is what happened to Megan."

The last few times she tried to face Megan with facts, it failed. Even watching the news report on dream advertising together did not convince her.  they were barely speaking now Holly did not see how she could even broach the subject.

She also wondered if she could go into Megan's room and break the smart pillow so it would not work anymore. Of course, Megan may never forgive her. Plus, Megan had started to lock her bedroom door the few times she did go out. A weird development for someone who has always been so open and free.

Instead, Holly thought her last hope was to get Megan out of the house and back into nature – and a social life.

Neither had much work the next few weeks. So, Holly tried to make plans for hiking, yoga on the red rocks of Sedona, concerts, and pub crawls. Megan did not go to all of them, but she was getting out of the house 3-4 times per week now.

They did not talk politics although Holly planned to volunteer for the Democratic presidential candidate Gloria Swindon. She would knock on doors and talk to people about the importance of voting. Arizona was a swing state where every vote counted and she knew it could even sway the entire national election.

As Megan got out of the house more, tensions in the house seemed to lift and things started to at least feel more normal. Perhaps the friendship was back on more solid ground.

One night toward the end of August, Holly came home to find Megan sobbing uncontrollably on the couch.

"What happened? What's wrong?" Holly asked.

Megan only cried louder and more intensely now.

"Please tell me". Holly pleaded.

Megan reached for a paper on the coffee table and handed it to Holly.

Holly saw it was a credit card bill and gasped. Her e grew open wide when she read the number; $27,649.

"Oh my God Megan." Holly said, her eyes still open wide.

"Is it all those Sheimu boxes?" Holly asked.

Megan cried even harder and nodded her head. Her sense of shame and anguish were palpable.

Holly sat next to her on the couch and hugged her roommate tight. Holly began crying too.

They sat and hugged for the longest time.

Finally, Megan tried to speak and sobbed. "What am I going to do? I don't know how I can ever pay that off."

Holly thought for a moment and said "you can send it all back. At least most of it. I mean, you haven't even opened half of these."

"You think?" Megan asked.

"It's gotta be worth a shot" Holly said.

"I've never had debt in my life, why would I even do this? Megan asked.

"Megan, it's not your fault. It's that damned pillow" Holly said.

"Yeah?" Megan asked.

"This all started after you bought that stupid pillow. They have been advertising to you in your dreams and this is what happens." Holly said softly, trying to soften the blow.

Megan stared at the wall.

"You need to throw that thing away" Holly said. "Otherwise, the next bill could be twice that much." She wanted to mention Megan's changed political views as well but figured that would be too much for her to take right now.

"OK, but how will I get to sleep?" Megan asked.

"The same way you did before, by getting exercise and laying off the electronics before you lay down or smoke some weed. Anything but using that manipulation pillow." Holly answered.

Megan went to her room and brought the smart pillow back to the living room. "Wanna help me wreck this thing?" She asked. Holly smiled and nodded.

They put the pillow on the floor. Then, they took turns stomping on it until they were sure the electronics inside were broken. They laughed and stomped and then opened a bottle of wine.

The next day, Megan started to print return labels for the Sheimu boxes. She felt overwhelmed because it would take weeks to send most of it back. And well into September the delivery trucks arrived to take things away and not to deliver them. After a few weeks, she was able to reduce her credit card debt to $16,000  not every item could be returned.

Holly had started canvassing for the upcoming election. She hoped Megan would join her, as she had in the past.

"Hey, do you want to help me cover Sunnyside tonight?" Holly asked.

Megan pondered the question and replied "ah, not feeling it this year."

"C'mon, they want to roll back women's rights and put migrants in cages. We need to do what we can." Holly said.

"Oh, I'm not sure its that bad." Megan replied.

Stunned, Holly replied. "So, you still think that way?"

"Kinda, yeah. It's all so confusing now and I'm not sure what to believe" Megan replied.

Crestfallen, Holly took her bike and outside and headed for the Sunnyside neighborhood.

As autumn progressed, the presidential election became all that anyone could talk about. Pelley and his surrogates kept making outrageous statements about immigrants. They even said that God did not want them in the country.

Holly gently tried to work on Megan, whose radically changed beliefs seemed to be softening but there still seemed to be a lingering distrust of immigrants. Megan and Holly still went to the same parties. Megan again voiced support for women's issues. But, she no longer spoke up about immigration.

By early November, the election was at a fever pitch. Everyone in deep blue Flagstaff was hoping the Democratic strongholds of Tucson, Flagstaff, and Tempe could sway Arizona for their candidate, Gloria Swindon. The polls showed her neck and neck with Pelley.

Election night came at last. Holly went to a rally to watch the results with Cassandra, Kelly, and other party volunteers. Megan stayed home. The group sipped on beer and watched the east coast results start to roll in which showed a very tight race. Swindon was clearly winning the popular vote, but Pelley had an edge in the Electoral College. The central time zone results mostly favored Pelley with Texas, Missouri, Kansas, Oklahoma, and others voting red. Swindon picked up Illinois, Wisconsin, and Minnesota.

Everyone knew the big west coast states would all go blue. So, Swindon still had a chance. She'd need to win swing states Colorado, Nevada, and Arizona to pull it off. The race was down to the wire. The gathering of Coconino County Democrats hoped they had done enough this time to deliver a strong showing to help Swindon win.

Then the TV announcer said that Colorado and New Mexico were called for Swindon and cheers rang out in the hall. There was still hope.

The Arizona returns were very tight. The lead changed by tiny margins as each county's returns came in. The more populated Phoenix area took the longest to count. Almost every county had already started a mandatory recount since the margins were so close.

By now Holly and her fellow volunteers were exhausted. This would take all night.

Later, Nevada was called for Swindon by a tiny margin. This left Swindon and Pelley within five electoral votes of each other. Whoever would win Arizona and its 11 Electoral College votes would be the President of the United States.

Finally, by 2 AM the final tally came in and the hall went silent. Pelley had won Arizona by just 16 votes and with it, victory in the 2024 US Presidential election. The Christian Nationalist Party even barely won the popular vote since so fewer Democrats turned out to vote this year. The Christian Nationalist Party also won control of the Senate and the House of Representatives by a small margin.

Sobs and tears filled the hall, and Cassandra started to talk about her worst fears of what would happen next. Pelley had promised a nationwide abortion ban. He also planned to deport over 11 million immigrants. He would put them into camps before shipping them out. Some of his party leaders even talked about banning birth control.

Pelley's plans also included firing most federal civil servants. He would replace them with his own loyalists. He would also change the US legal code to better fit "Christian ideals."

Holly sat stunned and could barely move. What would she do now? Would any woman in America feel safe now? She, Kelly, and Cassandra all shared teary hugs then Holly sat with her own grief.

She lacked enough money to move to Europe. Even though her friends in the UK and Greece were always asking her to come over. Maybe she could live in Mexico?

Kelly asked her if she needed a ride, but she declined while sitting in a daze. At around 3:30 AM she picked herself up and started a long walk home. The cold mountain air bit at her ears and eventually she made it to her street and saw the lights on in the house.

She opened the door, shook off the cold, and hung up her coat. She then walked into the living room. Megan was sitting in stunned silence with tears running down her cheeks. Pundits on the TV were talking about the election and what they think will happen next.

Megan looked up at Holly with a pained look on her face and said,

"I didn't even vote."

*In 2013, the first patent for a pillow to monitor brain waves was granted to a Chinese company.*

*In 2020, the Dormio study at the Massachusetts Institute of Technology (MIT) successfully proved methods to alter the content of dreams.*

*In 2021, an American Marketing Association survey indicated that 75% of US marketing firms aim to deploy dream advertising technologies by 2025.*

*In 2023, Apple was granted a patent for placing EEG monitors in Airpods.*

*Today, neurotechnology enabled sleep aid wearables and smart pillows are already available to consumers.*

# CHAPTER TWO

# CONDOTTIERI FLEET

*The Condottieri were Italian mercenary leaders who commanded bands of professional soldiers during the late Middle Ages and Renaissance. They were hired by city-states, monarchs, and popes to conduct warfare on their behalf. They often switched allegiances based on who could offer them the largest payoff or other political advantages.*

### Gulf of Aden

Floating like a ghost ship in the early morning mist, the long sleek grey vessel *Charybdis* showed no signs of life. A few minutes later, large doors on its deck slid open and methodically launched 14 armed drones, each carrying a pair of air-to-surface missiles.

Their targets were the drone and missile launch sites near Sanaa in Houthi-held Yemen which had been attacking commercial shipping in the Red Sea again after a three-year hiatus. An additional 28 drones were launched from the *Bahamut* and the *Scylla*, the *Charybdis'* sister ships in the Red Sea. Fifteen minutes later, the doors on the deck slid opened again and launched two reconnaissance drones behind the first wave to assess the results of the raid.

Once these drones were launched, the *Charybdis* and her sister vessels moved to offset locations to reduce the chance of a Houthi counterstrike. Despite these vessels' ample air defense capabilities, such precautions were always taken.

A little more than an hour later, multiple Houthi drone and missile sites and command centers were struck. Back at the control center, Giulia Rovigo, executive commander of the fleet, took a sip of coffee and asked for an update. Her demeanor was that of a coiled spring and her light brown hair was pulled into a tight bun.

"Yes ma'am" replied the watch officer, a former Philippine coast guard officer. "We should recover all but two drones since they malfunctioned and had to be ditched at sea. We're still waiting for all the damage assessments but so far we can confirm 23 surface-to-surface missile launchers, 14 long range drones, and one command center are damaged and inoperable."

Without her face changing expression, Giulia replied, "OK, let me know when we've confirmed the rest. I'm off to call the boss." She then strode out of the command center and up a short flight of stairs to the top deck of a refitted super-yacht and into her stateroom which overlooked the azure waters off the eastern coast of Crete. Her space was spartan, with barely any furnishing and all her belongings could fit into two suitcases. Since her boss could send her anywhere in the world for weeks at a time, it paid to live and travel light.

The super-yacht, 120 meters long, was a gift from the government of the United Arab Emirates (UAE) which allowed the fleet to base in the country in exchange for protection *in extremis*. The company also had a similar deal with Egypt and was in talks with two Southeast Asian governments for similar arrangements.

Giulia took a glass of water before sitting down to call her boss, Basil Kostatakis, on a secure videophone to report on today's raid. She didn't like to make such calls in the operations center, since she didn't want the watch officers to be privy to their deliberations.

Basil's face came onto the screen and in clinical fashion, Giulia began her report. "Everything is functioning normally, and we recovered 40 of 42 drones. Of course we can bill the Saudis for two we lost."

"Why not bill Brussels as well" Basil smirked, referring to the mission also being funded by the European Union, Japan, and India. Giulia remained stone-faced.

"What about the results today?" Basil asked.

Giulia's 25 years in the Italian Navy taught her to always report a mission's outcome first but Basil preferred to know the status of the fleet before anything else.

She replied "we have damage assessments on about half the sites and still need some analysis on the rest. We may need to send another reconnaissance mission to confirm some things on a drone site since one command center still may be operable."

"Alright, call me when you can confirm the rest." Basil said and signed off without even a goodbye.

Giulia let out a long breath then headed back down to the command center to await final confirmation. Once her final report was in, this mission would end a six-month billing cycle. The fleet would invoice its sponsors and start to send its vessels to Egypt to refuel and rearm. They would return only only once the invoices were all paid, and a new mission was funded.

She left her deputy in charge of the remaining tasks then walked out to the helipad on the front deck of the command ship *Amphitrite* and boarded a helicopter bound for the resort town of Vouliagmeni on the Athens Riviera. They needed to land before the temperature got too hot for it to safely fly since the summers had become unbearable. She would arrive just in time for a massage and a late brunch.

### Nicosia, Cyprus

It was a Monday morning and Alex Stavrou put down his coffee cup after reading the latest intelligence report from KYP, Cyprus' national intelligence service. He sat for a minute and rubbed his brow as he thought about how they would present this information to the president.

He called the president's personal secretary and informed them he had an urgent matter to discuss with the president, head of KYP, minister of defense, minister of foreign affairs, and minister of energy. This matter was too sensitive for a full meeting of the national security council, and he could not afford any leaks.

Alex had only been the national security advisor for nine months now, but it had been a baptism by fire. The 2024 election of Pelley in the United States had set off a chain reaction of events which were reshaping the global order.

In early 2025, the US stopped supporting Ukraine which enabled Russia to seize more territory in the south, all the way to Odessa and into Moldova. This left the EU to support a severely hobbled Ukraine which, while they continued to fight, was no longer economically viable. This proved to be tricky for an EU that was simultaneously working to re-arm after decades of neglect. Russia had also re-positioned its fleet to replace the vessels of its Black Sea Fleet which Ukraine had destroyed since 2022.

Since the Georgian government had moved even closer to Moscow since 2023, Russian troops were once again stationed in the country near the capital, ostensibly to"protect" the Baku-Tbilisi-Ceyhan (BTC) gas pipeline.

The BTC pipeline which had been designed to bypass Russia, was now under Russian influence. Moscow had its hand on the spicket once again and needed to drive up energy prices to finance its recovery after years of being battered by Western economic sanctions.

The EU was still in the process of re-arming and was now focused on defending central and southern Europe from possible future Russian incursions. Relations with Turkey continued to sour as their prospects for EU membership had faded to near zero, leading Ankara to join Brazil, Russia, India, China, South Africa, and Iran in BRICS.

In Washington, Pelley doubled down on US support for Israel which alienated Turkey and the Middle East. His son-in-law developing seized beachfront properties on Gaza's coastline was among the steps which closed the door to any chances for future rapprochement. This served as a final untethering from the west which led Ankara into the arms of Moscow and an energy partnership to control a larger part of the global gas market.

So, in addition to its own significant gas discoveries in the Black Sea, Turkey was now doing their part alongside Russia to squeeze the Ceyhan end of the BTC pipeline and extract higher fees from companies shipping gas through it.

Turkey remained a member of NATO but since the US had largely disengaged from it, the venerable military alliance was adrift and only marginally useful to anyone. There was some talk of the EU buying key NATO command centers and AWACS aircraft, but Pelley's team was driving a hard bargain, wanting to scrape back as much as they could from their share of NATO before it completely dissolved.

Making matters even worse, six months ago Turkey annexed the unrecognized Turkish Republic of Northern Cyprus. Since no other country in the world recognized it, a referendum was held in occupied Cyprus to join Turkey, a vote which passed with 71% saying yes. Any chance of reunifying the island had been dashed.

Just before lunch that day, Alex was ushered into the president's office along with the KYP director and the ministers of defense, energy, and foreign affairs.

KYP started the briefing. Under the watchful eye of his director, a former Cypriot army intelligence officer presented a series of slides and stood in front of a large map of Cyprus and the Eastern Mediterranean.

"Mister President, we received intelligence from MI-6 yesterday that Turkey and Russia are planning to seize the gas and oil platforms in our exclusive economic zone (EEZ) under the false premise that they are illegally operating in the Turkish EEZ."

Tension filled the room as the briefer continued.

"We verified what we could through our own sources and also learned that Turkey and Russia are planning joint maritime exercises to commence 2-3 months from now. This could be their cover for these alleged plans."

The president asked, "How confident are you in this information?"

The briefer continued. "Our observations of the Turkish fleet and special forces are operating at a higher state of readiness and conducting rehearsals which indicate this intel may be correct."

The minister of foreign affairs bolted up in her seat and asked, "what sort of rehearsals?"

The KYP director now took over from the briefer and replied, "We were not certain for some weeks after this information was shared by the Romanians, since we thought the Turks were rehearsing for the protection of energy platforms in the Black Sea. But if we are to believe the British report from yesterday, then perhaps these are not rehearsals to protect such platforms but to seize them."

The whole room went silent, then was bursting with questions.

The president asked, "Will they invade us on land as well?"

The KYP director replied, "We have no indications they are preparing for such actions,but they could attack our key radars and communications nodes as part of any action to seize the energy platforms."

The president turned to the minister of defense and asked, "how can we stop them?"

The defense minister dryly replied. "Sir, without a lot of help, we will be unable to deter them. We have sufficient forces to protect our territory and perhaps only 2-3 of the 14 blocks but if we get into a shooting war with combined Turkish and Russian naval forces it will be too great a challenge."

"Won't the British help us as part of the basing agreement?" The president asked.

"Yes sir, in theory they can assist with air and maritime forces, but it still will not be sufficient. Also, since Russia is in the mix it's not clear if the Labour government in the UK will be keen on getting into a standoff against Russia."

"What about the Americans? Exxon-Mobil has the contract in block Glaucus-1 so they won't want the Turks and Russians to seize that will they?"

"They've been heavily committed to the Taiwan straits this past year so they may not be able to help us much, even if they wanted to" replied the defense minister.

This time the energy minister spoke up, "For all we know, the Turks and Russians may have given assurances to Pelley that Exxon will keep the contract but now the fees go to Turkey and not us. I can't imagine this has not already been part of their calculus to take Washington off the board."

The president said, "Yes, with Pelley everything can be bought." He then asked the group, "is there anyone we can count on?"

"Israel and Egypt have always had our backs on these matters, but they may be more concerned about their own energy platforms in this situation. I will talk to them and see." The foreign minister replied.

"No, not yet" the president snapped at her. "We need to figure this out before we risk any leaks. We need to keep our options open."

The energy minister spoke up, "The French may be our best bet right now. Total has the contract for the Cronus gas field and the French navy has been making presence patrols there every year. Then of course there is Greece and the Italians."

"OK, that is a good start" the president said. He turned to the minister of foreign affairs and said, "Eleni, I need you find out if Paris, Athens, and Rome can help us." He then turned toward Alex and said, "Who else, what about the EU?

"I was planning to call them right after this. The new EU maritime command has had great challenges in generating forces tp conduct regional and global patrols since the Americans pulled back."

The defense minister added, "the northern EU member states seem very busy deterring the Russians in the Baltic, North, and Arctic Seas so it may be down to just our friends in the neighborhood."

The president said "I will call Mixalis tonight" referring to Cyprus' permanent representative to the EU. He then continued, "Alex, I want you to help him and see what the EU can do for us.They are always talking about this toolbox so let's see if it can help us to protect our territory, our gas fields and our economy."

He started to turn away then turned back to Alex and said, "Remind them we need them to act fast or this could be over before it even starts."

The president then stood up and faced the defense minister. "I want you to discreetly start to prepare our forces. We can't give them any indication that we know what they are planning."

The defense minister replied "We'll be as discreet as we can, but some actions can't be so easily hidden. I think if we talk about this internally as responding to the upcoming naval exercises it will be believable and not completely tip our hand. In fact, if we can gather any additional forces to assist us, it should be under the guise of our own maritime exercises."

The president nodded, "I like this approach, do it."

"Now everyone go and get started. I will see you all back here in 6 hours." With thatt he president dismissed the group.

Alex went back downstairs, pulled his mobile phone out of the secure box and walked across the hallway to text his wife Marietta their code word that he would be home very late tonight.

He then returned to his office, put his mobile phone back in the box, and picked up the secure line to call Cyprus' ambassador to the EU, but he put the phone down since he did not want to get ahead of the president. So instead, Alex thought it better to call Astrid, his counterpart at the European Council. They had been classmates during a course at the European Security and Defense College 10 years earlier and they worked together quite a bit during Cyprus' recent turn in the rotating EU Presidency.

He knew his government was about to kick off something big and he was glad to be able to talk it over with someone he knew who could help them to choreograph the first steps in this crisis.

### Justus Lipsus Building, Brussels
### European Council Secretariat

Astrid Rikard had been preparing papers for tomorrow's meeting of the EU's Peace and Security Council when the secure phone rang. She put down her coffee and answered the phone.

"Hi Astrid, its Alex. Your old friend in Nicosia."

"Hi Alex, it's nice to hear from you. How is Marietta? Are you in town this week?" Astrid replied.

"She is fine thanks. And no, I am not in Brussels, but I may be soon since we have a serious situation here." Alex said.

Astrid twisted her face a bit which she was glad Alex could not see. Cyprus was often bringing up some kind of crisis be it a Turkish oil exploration ship in their waters or some kind of harassment coming from their neighbors to the north. It was never seen as a priority in Brussels, but she admired the Cypriots persistence to keep attention on these situations.

"What is it now Alex?" Astrid said, trying not to sound bored.

"We have indications that Turkey and Russia may try to seize the gas platforms in our exclusive economic zone within the next few months." Alex said.

Astrid drew in a breath and replied "Are you sure Alex? What sources are telling you this?"

"It comes from a friendly government and is confirmed as far as we can by our own sources and those of another member state. I can send you more when I write up the summary." Alex said.

"So that friendly government is not an EU member state?" Astrid asked.

"No, but they used to be." Alex quipped (indicating the intelligence came from the British). He was crossing a line by sharing so much already but he needed Astrid onboard.

"Ah, OK." Astrid replied. Knowing the source was the UK gave her some comfort and a tinge of pain. Being the daughter of an English mother and a Swedish father, it still pained her that the UK had left the EU.

"So how do you want to proceed?" Astrid asked.

Alex said, "I think we are looking at a request to declare an Article 42, paragraph seven situation in order to deter Turkey and Russia from this plan." He was referring to the EU's mutual defense clause which It had only been used once in 2015 after the terror attacks in Paris – and even then, it did not involve the commitment of EU military forces.

"OK, that is a big one Alex" Astrid replied.

"We may also request to declare Article 222, the Solidarity Clause. Can we ask for both at the same time?" Alex inquired.

"Anything is possible" Astrid said and continued, "Article 42 (7) may allow for us to activate some military capabilities and help generate forces for deterrence, but it would also be the first time the EU would be in a possible armed standoff."

Alex replied, "yes, I understand that. But the Solidarity Clause also provides funding and other instruments to help us too."

"Alex, the Solidarity Clause has only been used for natural disasters and such and no disaster has happened yet. This could be tricky." Astrid said.

"So, we must first wait until we are attacked or invaded to get that kind of help? C'mon, we are the major gas producer inside the EU." Alex said, sounding exasperated.

"I don't mean it like that Alex, I mean it's just never been done like this before." Astrid said in a conciliatory tone. She added, "But this sounds like a situation where it's needed"

"OK, thanks Astrid." Alex said, "Our ambassador will be calling the PSC chair soon so now you'll be ready."

"Thanks for the advance warning." Astrid said.

Alex replied, "I'll call you tomorrow when we know more."

They both hung up the phones and got to work. Alex called Cyprus' new ambassador to the EU, Mixalis Costas, and discussed how to approach requesting the activation of the mutual defense and solidarity clauses of the EU treaty. The ambassador listened but seemed annoyed that Alex was explaining so much of it. Everyone was treating him like he was in primary school and neither he, nor his pride, liked it one bit. He bit his tongue as Alex explained that for any request, they would need to produce a supporting situation and intelligence report which would require asking MI-6 if they can release the intelligence the British shared with Cyprus to the rest of the EU. Mixalis noted in a bitter tone that any such report would need to be produced in Nicosia, not in Brussels.

Alex agreed profusely. "Of course, Mister Ambassador, and we'll need your blessing on any final draft." This seemed to assuage Mixalis, for now.

With the atmosphere on the call more balanced now, Alex informed Mixalis what actions Nicosia would be taking in the coming hours and days.

"For any mutual defense request, the MOD will need to develop a list of the force capabilities we'd need, in what numbers, and how they would be employed to defend Cyprus." Alex said.

The ambassador replied, "Would the MOD want to lead the mission themselves or would it be better to have an EU force commander?"

By the time Alex hung up the phone, he had a long checklist of questions from the ambassador in addition to his own.

Meanwhile, Astrid started digging up records from 2015 on how France requested the activation of the mutual defense clause and the times the solidarity clause has been activated so she'd be armed with all the procedures and precedents when the Cypriot ambassador called her boss that night. And that call came much sooner than expected.

Stefan Wouters had been the chairman of the European Union's Peace and Security Committee (known as the PSC in Brussels circles) for close to six years. So, he was used to taking such calls from member states, especially in the years since Russia's full-scale invasion of Ukraine in 2022. About 30 minutes later, Ambassador Mixalis Costas and a member of his staff came to his office and spent an hour inside behind closed doors before quietly leaving at around 6pm.

Wouters then had Astrid place phone calls to the Chief of Staff of the European External Action Service, the Chief of the EU Military Staff, and head of the EU's Intelligence Centre to come to his office for a meeting that night.

### Presidential Palace, Nicosia

The president entered the room last and started asking his first question before he even sat down at the head of the table.

"So, Eleni, what news from our friends?" he asked the foreign minister.

"Mister president, Athens responded positively, and they will see what kind of maritime support they can send to help us."

The defense minister cleared his throat, causing the president to nod to him.

The defense minister spoke up. "Mister president, while of course Athens will support us, we need to be realistic about how much they can help us. As you know, they have their own challenges now dealing with Libya and Turkey in their waters south of Crete, so their hands are quite full already."

"Hmmm "the president said, then he turned back to the foreign minister and asked, "OK Eleni, what about the others?"

The foreign minister continued "Paris supports us completely and will send us at least two ships. They will also strongly support us at the EU level."

The president perked up at this news and said, "that is quite positive, what about Rome?"

She continued, "the Italians also offered their support at the EU level, but they are not sure how much they can help us since they are already leading the force in the Red Sea." She then turned to the defense minister looking for support.

The defense minister took a deep breath and spoke, "Sir, the Italian carrier Garibaldi and two other vessels were damaged by Houthi missile strikes so their operational reserve may be quite thin"

The president nodded then turned to Alex, "what is the word from Brussels?"

"Mister president, we have a good case for an article 42, paragraph seven declaration which could help lead to an EU maritime force to help us, provided Hungary and Slovakia don't veto it. We also may have grounds for invoking the Solidarity clause, which would provide us some broader types of support and perhaps some funding. But it could be tricky." Alex said.

"Ambassador Costas mentioned some of that a little while ago. Tricky how," the president asked.

"It could be tricky because the Solidarity clause has only been used after emergencies like natural disasters, never something like this" Alex responded.

The president let out a long breath and looked down at the table in anger. "I hope they realize the EU standing to lose one of its only internal sources of energy is an emergency."

"I think they will see this mister president" Alex replied.

The president looked up through his glasses at Alex and said, "OK, I also want you to call the Americans and see if they can help us.

"I will do that mister president" Alex said.

The president then turned to the defense minister.

"Mister president, I have placed our navy and special operations forces on a higher level of readiness while the army and air force are only stepping up on a few measures which are not so easily detected. Our general staff is working on an operational plan to deter Turkey and Russia and defining what size and type of force it would take to do so." The defense minister reported. "What we know so far is that we can't achieve deterrence alone. One question is that if the EU takes on such a mission, who leads which parts of the operation"

The president asked, "Is there any precedent for this kind of arrangement?"

"Yes, when we had the EU Operation Sophia during the first migration crisis, the EU commanded one part of the operation and the Italians commanded their national mission in parallel. So, this is nothing new" the defense minister said.

"OK, tomorrow night I want a detailed briefing from you on our defense posture and how the plan is coming along. I want something concrete by Thursday so I can start calling my counterparts" the president said before turning to the KYP director.

"Any updates from the UK? Will they allow us to release this intelligence so we can request declarations from the EU and any other help we need?

The KYP director responded, "Yes mister president. We are working on a semi-sanitized version of the intelligence that London should agree on. I should have a response by noon tomorrow."

"OK, very good". The president said. "Now everyone go home and get a good night's sleep. It going to be a long week." He then left the room.

The rest of the Cyprus national security council looked at each other in silence then shuffled out of the room. Once outside the room the KYP director and defense minister stopped to chat at the top of the stairs while the others made their way down to the foyer and out the door past the presidential guards.

**Brussels**

Astrid had prepared a briefing paper for the meeting which was still short on details since the Cypriots only provided two paragraphs on the situation, but it was enough to get started on the big strategic questions.

Just before 8pm, the head of the EU military staff, Gianfranco Nunzio, and a few key staff from the European External Action service and EU intelligence center (INTCEN) filed into Stefan Wouters' conference room. By now they had all read the classified email that invited them to this meeting, so the briefing paper was a formality.

Wouters opened up the meeting with his usual easy manner, which quickly shifted to a more serious tone.

"First off, INTCEN, do we have any way to verify or corroborate what the Cypriots are telling us?"

The INTCEN chief, Klara Linder, had come up through the ranks of Swedish intelligence so she was not one of the ambitious dilettantes that seem to dominate many of the EU institutions. Instead, she was a rarity in Brussels, a professional who deeply knew her craft.

She replied, "We do have some corroborating intelligence, but I'll have to ask the member states for updated reporting which would be more specific."

"Have you done so yet?" asked Wouters.

"Given the sensitivity of this situation and the alarm such inquiries could trigger in some member states, I wanted to get some guidance on that from the High Representative before proceeding" Klara said.

"A wise decision since I've not yet had a chance to fully brief her," replied Wouters.

He then turned to the group and said, "The Cypriots are intending to ask for an Article 42 (7) and Article 222 declarations. So, what options do we have?"

One EEAS official spoke up, "well, we should start with sanctions"

He was quickly cut off by Wouters who said, "the Commission is looking at that in parallel. We're here to talk about other measures." He then turned his gaze to the Director General of the EU Military Staff.

Vice Admiral Nunzio cleared his throat and said "Mr. Chairman, we've developed military missions before but never one that involves a possible military confrontation. Our staff is certainly competent to develop such a plan, but my concern is force generation; who will provide the ships and other capabilities we need?"

Wouters face twisted, "are you saying that with all the powerful navies we have, we may not have enough of a force to do the job?"

The admiral took in a deep breath, "Mr. Chairman, we have an active mission in the Red Sea that has been going on for three years now so there are not exactly a lot of vessels in the member states that are ready to deploy so fast."

Nunzio turned to his aide who handed him an index card. The admiral began to read. "The Italian carrier Cavour may be available in about 12-14 weeks, since it is still in a maintenance cycle. As you know, the other Italian carrier, Garibaldi, just pulled into Taranto to repair damage from a Houthi missile strike during operations in the Red Sea"

Wouters and the others took a deep breath as the admiral continued to speak, "Italy also has three frigates committed to the Libyan Sea to support Greece since Turkey and Libya have been threatening their oil and gas platforms there aswell."

"What about France?" Wouters asked.

"The Charles de Gaulle has been in a deep maintenance cycle after a long mission in the Pacific, so it won't be available for another 4-6 months. France does have three frigates and two battalions of marines ready for deployment within 3-5 weeks."

The admiral continued, "getting back to Greece, we project they have 1-2 frigates and two SEAL teams with their own special operations vessels within the same time frame."

"From the rest, we estimate Spain and Croatia may have some assets available, but the staff is only starting the coordination process." Admiral Nunzio concluded with a sigh.

Astrid slipped a note to her boss Wouters with a question on it that read "what size and kind of force do we need to deter Turkey and Russia?"

Wouters nodded in agreement to Astrid, glad he had someone on his team with who asked the questions no one else did.

"Admiral, has your staff yet worked out what size and type of force we'd need to deter Turkey and Russia from seizing Cyprus' oil and gas platforms?" Wouters asked.

"Not yet sir, but the last time we exercised anything similar to this we needed more than 18 large surface ships to include two air defense vessels, plus 1-2 submarines and air support. The staff is working on an estimate now in coordination with the Cypriot MOD, he responded.

Wouters put his hands under his glasses and rubbed his eyes and said, "it sounds like we're going to be well short of that number."

"Quite possibly sir, yes, Admiral Nunzio replied.

"What about the UK? Don't they have a defense agreement with Cyprus?" an EEAS staffer asked.

Nunzio turned to the back bencher then back to Wouters, "yes they do but we don't keep track of their readiness anymore since they left the EU."

A member of Nunzio's staff spoke up "sir, I will check on that tonight. One thing we do know is that the British currently have a carrier and a destroyer committed to a NATO mission in the high north alongside the Norwegian and Swedish navies shadowing the Russian northern fleet."

Wouters let out a long exhalation, "the timing of this is...."

"Quite bad and seems to be intentional" Klara added.

"What about the Americans? Can they or will they do anything?"

"Even if they wanted to, the US fleet is quite busy trying to keep China from invading Taiwan. The best we can hope for is some intelligence support" Nunzio said.

From the back bench someone spoke under their breath "they are probably happy since gas prices will be higher."

One of Admiral Nunzio's staff officers leaned toward him and whispered, "what about calling Mister Kostatakis?" The admiral glared at the officer and motioned for him to lean back to his back bench chair.

Wouters put his hands together in front of him and thought for a moment.

"OK, I want to see everyone in here at 5pm tomorrow night for an update briefing and. I need solid options. I will be speaking with the High Representative and the Cypriot ambassador again tonight." Wouters concluded and then dismissed the group.

As they all filed out, Max Blank, an officer from the EU Military Staff nodded to Astrid that he wanted to chat with her. Astrid met Max at a party two years ago and they played tennis together a few times, but nothing ever came of it. Still, they remained on friendly terms.

Max was a tall navy officer from the northern Bavaria region of Franconia. He grew up about as far from the coast as a German could but after learning how to windsurf as a teenager, he fell in love with the sea. He eventually found his way to the northern German island of Sylt where he learned to sail and surf. Not satisfied with such small craft, he shocked all his hippie surfing friends when he applied to the German naval academy.

Now 22 years later he was in Brussels and shocked that he seemed to be the only one who knew how to solve the problem facing Cyprus and the EU.

Astrid took Max to her office and left the door open.

"How have you been Max?" she asked.

"Fine, fine," he said. "I have an idea."

"What kind of idea?" Astrid asked.

"An idea to solve the problem with this situation," Max replied.

"You think you can talk Russia and Turkey out of this?" she asked impishly.

"No silly, to get the forces we need. We rent them." Max said.

"Oh no Max, not those robot mercenaries" Astrid responded. "I thought of them too but asking them to go against the Houthis is not the same as asking them to help against two powerful states. Do you have any idea how hard that was to get agreement on for the Red Sea? Ugh. The price would be astronomical."

"Maybe, but we don't know unless we ask," Max replied. "Plus," he went on "we're only asking them to help us deter so they may not even have to fight."

"Hmmm, but that's a slippery slope if we aren't careful. Maybe they'd charge us to help protect Cyprus,then run off if shooting started. Either way, I don't think we'd ever get member states to agree on it again" Astrid pondered.

Just then, Wouters poked his head in Astrid's door.

"What's this all about?" Wouters asked.

Astrid, regretting that she'd left her door open, responded, "Just catching up with a friend."

Not satisfied with the answer, Wouters stood in silence.

Max was not prepared to brief the chairman of the EU Peace and Security Committee on his idea, especially without his boss (or his boss's boss) approving.

"We used to play tennis and I wanted to see if Astrid would join me again sometime,"Max said.

Seemingly satisfied but now a bit perturbed, Wouters responded "who can think of tennis at a time like this?" He then turned and left.

"Whew, that was close" Astrid said.

Max looked pale and nodded his head.

She then said to Max, "if you really think this is a good idea, then have your boss make it one of the options at the briefing tomorrow night."

Thinking of how to suggest it to his superiors, Max shook his head and said "Ok, I'll do my best."

Before leaving for the night, Astrid picked up her secure phone again to call Alex and see how he reacted to Max's idea. No one answered his line, so she sent him a one-line email on the secure system. All it said was "can Basil K.help?"

### Nicosia

Alex did not sleep well after the long and busy Monday. He was not there to say good night to his young children, Stavros and Klio. Marietta saved dinner for him which he ate, then went to sleep.

He knew today would be crucial since the buzz about their predicament would start to spread in the capital by the end of the week, regardless of how hard they tried to keep it secret. Too many people talk and divulge things they shouldn't, mostly to show off and look important to their friends. So, they had to be on top of the situation to maintain control and not lose precious time to prepare their defenses.

He opened his email account and found the usual press releases and unclassified reports, none of which interested him this morning. He then switched over to his classified email system and saw a note from Astrid with no subject line.

He then opened it and saw her short message. He was going to need a lot more coffee this morning.

The fact that she suggested even considering seeking help from Basil Kostatakis' Argonaut Marine told him the EU's internal meetings last night did not produce many viable options.

Alex had to think quickly on how he could bring up this idea to president and defense minister. First off, who would pay for it? Secondly, how long would this crisis last? If it was long enough, this single cost alone could break their national budget. Would they fall under an EU command or under the armed forces of Cyprus? Of course, that probably depended on who pays the bills.

Alex sent a note to KYP and military intelligence to jointly produce an analysis on the capabilities and limitations of Kostatakis' robot fleet and to have it ready by 5pm that day. It was a tall order on short notice but if he had to discuss this with the boss, he wanted to be ready.

During the day on Tuesday, Max managed to convince his EU Military Staff (EUMS) director to include Argonaut Marine as one of the options for the briefing that night. This in turn meant the options under discussion at the EU level were also shared with the Cypriot MOD staff and Alex as national security advisor. Alex was glad to be prepared but knew that tonight's discussions would be tense.

One EUMS staff officer had served with Giulia Rovigo, executive director of Argonaut Marine so he reached out to her to discreetly let her know to expect to be contacted soon by the EU for another possible job. Of course, he violated every security rule by contacting her but since he was nearing retirement, he wanted to win favor with Giulia and hopefully find a job in her organization.

### 22 Bishopsgate
### London

Giulia strode into the gleaming office tower and took the express elevator to Basil Kostatakis' executive suite on the 50th floor. His global headquarters took up two floors of the tower locally known as TwentyTwo.

She was glad not to live in this cold and rainy city, so she planned to make this a short visit. While she could have called or emailed her news to him, some things are best delivered in person, especially when you don't want certain governments to listen in.

An hour later she strode out of the building into a waiting taxi. She had a dull headache, probably from wearing her hair in a tight bun all day. She let her hair down as the taxi headed to Heathrow where she'd catch a flight to Dubai. The fleet may have a new and lucrative mission to prepare for so there was much work to be done. She had one nagging question though, would these potential new clients be willing to pay the price Basil had in mind?

### Nicosia

The national security council meeting that night started out tense. The defense minister reported out on preparations while the foreign ministry provided an update on their outreach to regional partners. The foreign minister asked again when she can share information about their predicament with Egypt and Israel, but the approvals were still not given.

"We're not sure we can trust them with this news yet and we still have not solidified our own plan, so the answer is not yet" said the president with a worn look on his face.

Finally, it was Alex's turn to report on his discussions with the EU on what options were on the table, including hiring Argonaut

Marine. The reactions were predictable; the defense minister was skeptical while the energy minister seemed open to the idea.

The president asked for more information about the Argonaut Marine option. Alex, glad to be prepared, turned to the KYP director and gave a nod for him to proceed.

The KYP director said, "Mister president, we have prepared a briefing for you on this already."

The president said, please proceed then."

The KYP director then motioned to a retired colonel who was sitting by a lectern who then stood up and began to speak while a screen behind him showed a series of slides and photos.

"Mister president, as you know, Basil Kostatakis is a dual Greek-UK citizen and one of the wealthiest men in the world having inherited the Argonaut shipping empire in his 20s," the briefer said.

He continued, "Since then, he has also diversified into investment banking which has more than doubled the value of his wealth. This is why he spends more time in London the past 20 years.

"OK, I know all of that, what about his fleet?" the president asked.

"Of course, mister president" the briefer replied. "Kostatakis started his own security company, Argonaut Marine, during the rise of sea piracy in the 2000s. He figured that instead of hiring others to protect his vessels, he would do it himself. He soon found that outside demand for this kind of security was high and began to add this to his portfolio of services."

The briefer continued, "Over the years since then, he has been outfitting some of his faster vessels for security missions and adding the latest technology to make them more effective and their services more marketable. More recently, this includes the ability to launch long range drones for both strike and reconnaissance."

The briefer went on, "Argonaut Marine has been hired by a consortium to provide security off east Africa to protect shipping during the insurgency in Mozambique, to stop illegal fishing in West Africa, and more recently they have been hired by a group of nations to strike Houthi targets from the Red Sea. They've also done several other missions in recent years."

The KYP director spoke up "According to some experts, Kostatakis seems to be competing with national navies – offering this company as a cheaper option, a navy for rent." He then motioned to the briefer to continue.

"In order to cut crew costs, he is now using artificial intelligence (AI) to takeover many functions of his Argonaut shipping fleet. This includes the Argonaut Marine vessels which have only a small crew of perhaps eight to twelve on each ship to handle command and control plus some maintenance functions. Until they can develop a maintenance robot, the crew size won't get much smaller." The briefer said.

After a quick pause to check his notes, the briefer continued, saying "He also now has a small submarine."

"The robot drone ships can launch both aerial and maritime drone swarms plus they have long range undersea drones. Each ship has its own air defense and electronic warfare capabilities and this year they may have acquired some cruise missiles in box launchers acquired through Egypt and the UAE."

The president's eyes opened wide. He knew Argonaut Marine had some special capabilities but had no idea they were so extensive.

"How big is this fleet and how is he legally able to function like this?" asked the president.

"Mister president, to your first question, the fleet consists of six surface combatants plus a resupply ship and the submarine I mentioned. By next year they should have seven surface ships plus an additional supply vessel," the briefer responded.

The defense minister spoke up "so they are potent but perhaps not such a very large force."

The briefer looked to his boss, the KYP director, before responding. "The numbers don't tell the whole story minister. We estimate that each Argonaut Marine vessel is so lethal that it may be counted as something closer to three conventional ships."

"So, they are like a fleet of 18? That can't be! That would make them as capable as some navies" the defense minister said.

"Precisely sir" The briefer responded.

"You still have not answered my second question, how are they legally able to operate this way?" the president asked.

This time the KYP director answered. "They have basing deals with Egypt and the UAE in exchange for protection by this fleet in crisis situations. These countries can also purchase ammunition and weapons that Argonaut Marine would normally not be able to buy as a private company. In many ways, they are a mercenary navy for those two countries plus anyone else who can afford to rent them."

"Ah, so that is how they are allowed to transit the Suez Canal with armed ships,"the foreign minister said.

The briefer responded, "yes minister, they also operate only in international waters or where they have specific permissions from the host nation to be underway armed."

The energy minister now had a question. "I still don't understand how this business model works. How can they afford to build and maintain such a fleet?"

Now it was Alex's turn to answer, since this was a topic he had studied for years. "Minister, Kostatakis already owned hundreds of vessels. But the main reason they can afford it is because the cost and access to this technology keeps getting lower, making more available to private and non-state actors. What was once something only states could do is now possible for people like Kostatakis."

The KYP director joined in, "Just look at Jeff Bezos and Elon Musk launching rockets into space. But for Kostatakis, while he may not make a large profit from Argonaut Marine, it gives him a seat at the table in ways that his wealth alone cannot. It gives him enormous leverage to shape events in ways that benefit his entire business empire."

The finance minister had been quiet throughout the last sessions of the national security council but finally spoke up. "And who would pay for this? Do we? The EU? And my other question is, can we afford it?"

**Brussels**

A similar briefing on the Argonaut Marine option had been conducted up in Brussels which resulted in many of the same questions with one addition. Was the EU equipped to manage a military confrontation that could tip over into a shooting war? Debates on addressing this question had raged in Brussels since the 2022 Russian full-scale invasion of Ukraine and since Pelley narrowly won the 2024 US presidential election and left NATO in tatters.

One problem Wouters and Nunzio wrestled with was that Article 42 (7) had never been used this way, but the provisions to operationalize it were still new and untested. Even the wording of the treaty provision stated that any such assistance would need to be organized bilaterally between the stricken nation and other EU member states, and not the EU itself. Of course, the European Council could still agree to launch an EU mission but without it being tethered to an existing treaty, it could leave an excuse for some member states to scuttle any agreement.

So, any EU-led assistance would need to lean heavily on Article 222 of the Treaty on the Functioning of the EU, also known as the Solidarity clause. This one allowed the EU to mobilize all instruments at its disposal, to include military forces and financial aid. The price tag for any such assistance in this case remained an unknown quantity.

### Brussels and Nicosia

A secure video teleconference was arranged between the EEAS and the Cypriot national security council to discuss how they would handle the impending threat to Cyprus. Lithuania, who held the rotating presidency of the EU, also took part.

The meeting started with an intelligence briefing by KYP, which had secured permission from the UK to share a sanitized version of the intelligence they had shared with Nicosia on the situation at hand. A number of participants in the meeting took in a deep breath during the conclusions portion, with Max turning to Astrid next to him on the back bench and whispering "things just got very real" to which she replied, "and scary."

Vice Admiral Nunzio, director of the EU military staff, presented a briefing on force requirements for a deterrence mission to protect Cyprus.

"Our estimates for such a mission are based on what size and type of force would be required to deter an estimate of what a combined Russian and Turkish force could looks like. So, we've had to err on the side of caution" Nunzio said.

He went on, "Now that our methodology is clear, our estimate indicates we'd need a force of 18 major surface vessels with air defense capabilities, 8-10 special forces teams, electronic warfare capabilities, plus two submarines and ample air cover to be provided from airfields in Cyprus."

The Cypriot defense minister spoke up, "or staffs have been working together on this estimate and we are in agreement with what Admiral Nunzio has presented."

Wouters asked to Nunzio, "Since we haven't heard back from all the member states yet, what size force do you think we can generate for this potential mission?"

Nunzio responded, "We think we can generate a force of nine major surface vessels, seven special forces teams, and one submarine. We think are in better shape at meeting the air force requirements with possible pledges from France, Sweden, Spain, and Greece plus whatever air support and special forces the UK provides in accordance with its treaty obligation to Cyprus."

Wouters seemed astonished, "I thought we had much more capacity than this."

Nunzio pondered a moment and replied, "Mister chairman, we can field twice this number,but these estimates are based on being able to maintain such a presence for 12 or more months, which means we must be able to rotate them every six months. So, this represents the size of force we can sustain there for a minimum of 12 months"

Alex spoke up, "So we have quite a gap between what we need and what we can generate. How can we close this gap?"

This time Wouters responded, "Alex, have you been able to reach out to Egypt or Israel yet?"

Alex responded, "Not yet, but we should very soon. What other options do you see?" He did not want to be the one to bring up the Argonaut Marine option.

"What about the Americans?" Wouters pressed.

"They said they were sorry they were too busy in the Indo-Pacific but did promise to provide intelligence support plus two surplus Mark V special operations craft for our special forces."

"Hmmph" Wouters grunted.

Wouters turned to Nunzio, who resented having to be the one to suggest hiring a private military company.

"As our staffs have discussed, there is also the option of hiring Argonaut Marine, but we would need to answer a number of questions first" Nunzio said.

"What questions?" Ambassador Costas asked.

"Firstly, do they have the specific capabilities we need, secondly, are our communications and targeting systems compatible, thirdly; what would the chain of command look like, and finally; what is the price and who would pay for it?" Nunzio recited from a list he was holding.

"And will the member states approve paying for it?" Wouters added.

The foreign minister Eleni Stylianidi, was first among equals on the Cypriot side so she transmitted the key message, "So, we need to work together to get answers to these questions as soon as possible."

Wouters responded, "Given the sensitivity of this situation, we'll need approval at the highest levels to proceed with any contact with Argonaut Marine."

"And so will we. We will seek that approval as soon as we finish this call, and our defense ministry will work with you on any technical details. Alex will also be available for any communications you have with Argonaut Marine," Eleni said.

"Very well" Wouters responded.

With that, the meeting ended. Wouters then turned to Astrid and said, "the high representative won't want to be too visible in this so any negotiations will fall to me."

That night Eleni contacted the president via a secure phone line and told him that if he would not let her seek support from Egypt and Israel at this point, she would tender her resignation. The president consented.

### Dubai

Two days later, Giulia took a call from Max inviting her to Brussels to speak with the EEAS. Max had served under Giulia during EU Operation Sophia in the Central Mediterranean and knew her to be a very smart and tough officer. She seemed to know the answer to any question before she asked it and he knew her to have sound integrity, even though she scared him a bit. Nonetheless, since he knew her already, he was tapped to make the first contact.

Giulia had been expecting the call, so she smiled when she heard Max's voice on the phone inviting her to Brussels. She agreed to be there in two days and asked for them to arrange for her to have a suite at the Stanhope Hotel not far from Place Luxembourg. After so many years of staying in tiny spaces on navy vessels, she only wanted luxury rooms when she traveled now. Besides, the EU would be paying anyway.

She sent a note off to Basil to let him know the dance of negotiation would be starting now and asked if the terms they discussed in London still stand. She then went down to the beach to get some sun during the late afternoon.

That night, she heard back from Basil wishing her good luck and telling her that his guidance on their negotiating position had not changed.

The next day she instructed her staff in Dubai to check on ammunition and supplies at their facility in Port Said, Egypt. All but one vessel was already in port for resupply, but the submarine was in the UAE, far from where the new mission would be. They were to get underway to Port Said within a week. She also told her technical team to see how fast they can repair and bring into operation all their electronic warfare capabilities and checked the status of the new cruise missile box launchers.

Late that night she boarded a plane and fell asleep in her reclined first-class seat, grateful that Emirates had a direct flight to Brussels.

### Nicosia

Having been volunteered by the foreign minister, Alex later found out he needed to fly to Brussels tomorrow for the first meeting with Argonaut Marine. He broke the news to Marietta that night who helped him pack his bag. The next morning, he kissed his children goodbye after breakfast and later squeezed into his economy class seat on flight to Athens, then onward to Brussels.

### Brussels

Alex arrived early to the Justus Lipsus building to meet with Astrid, Max, and other staffers to prepare for their first engagement with Giulia after lunch. Together they had tried to estimate what Argonaut Marine would charge for such a mission and under what conditions they would say yes.

In the last few days Klara Linder and the team at the EU Intelligence Center were able to complete a parallel reconstruction of the original UK report using information provided by member states. This meant the EU no longer needed to ask the UK for permission to release information related to the threat to Cyprus' energy platforms. This was especially important since any negotiation with Argonaut Marine would require the EU to share some information about the mission they were being considered for.

Max, Astrid, Alex, Klara, and the others concluded by lunch that Argonaut Marine would probably charge more for this kind of mission since it involves deterring two powerful states in Russia and Turkey. A requirement of four drone ships and one submarine was validated by the EU Military Staff and Cypriot MOD and the group estimated the price tag to be around 1-2 billion euros for six months. After lunch they would find out just how much they had underestimated the cost.

After landing in Brussels, Giulia checked into the Stanhope hotel, then she rode an exercise bicycle in the fitness room for an hour while she watched the news on the televisions mounted on the wall. Afterwards she got herself ready, had a nice breakfast, and got into a cab.

Clad in a black suit and low heels, Giulia strode into the place where she was to meet the EU staff members who had invited her. Since she could not be spotted entering any of the EU buildings without drawing attention, the meeting was set up at a large house in the suburb of Uccle, well away from the European Quarter.

Wearing a gray suit and not his uniform, Max greeted her at the door and took Giulia to the foyer. She seemed happy to see Max again and they chatted on the way inside. For security reasons, the EU had rented the house for the week. A few Belgian undercover police and intelligence personnel were on hand to make sure the meeting would not be eavesdropped on, having swept the building for bugs and setting up various electronic equipment to keep it secure.

Once inside, Giulia's hosts asked her to put her mobile phone into a box along with their own, then led her into the living room. A few of the EU staff, including Max, already knew Giulia so there were introductions all around as coffee was served around a standup table. To one side was also a long table with a gourmet buffet. "How civilized," Giulia said to herself.

The group chatted for about 20 minutes before Astrid beckoned them to the meeting table. Once sat around the table, Klara asked Giulia to sign a nondisclosure agreement before presenting her with a sanitized version of the intelligence report which started the whole thing.

Giulia nodded and asked a few knowing questions which left Klara wondering, "Either she already knew about this, or she is really smart."

Next, Max, Alex, and a Polish colleague Pawel Kowalski explained how they envisioned Argonaut Marine could help Cyprus and the EU in this situation by providing four drone carriers and submarine, along with the organic air defense, cruise missiles, and electronic warfare capabilities they needed. Giulia seemed more than ready for this discussion, talking about communications, logistics, and what the command-and-control arrangements would be. Pawel also told her they envisioned the mission to be for six months, possibly to be extended to 12 months or more.

Giulia had many questions, including what the rest of the force would comprise and what the concept for the operational plan would be. It was not lost on Alex or the EU staff that a private company now had almost the entire picture on a serious crisis being faced by Cyprus and the EU. Not even in the days of the pandemic was anything so serious shared with the private sector. They hoped they would not regret it.

One of the first conditions she voiced was that if Argonaut Marine decided to take on this mission, they would only report to the overall commander and not to any subordinate group commanders. They also would not just fill in other task forces but would be their own. Of course, Giulia smiled and told them, they were happy to have EU vessels assigned under their command if that was decided. Max and Pawel responded that legally no nation would allow its forces to be placed under the command and control of a private company, so this was out of the question.

She also turned to Alex and said, "We'd also need basing rights and support in Cyprus to even consider this."

"Of course," Alex replied. "I think our MOD was expecting this kind of request."

The group took a break which allowed Giulia and Alex to have a cordial discussion about basing arrangements in the kitchen while the others filled their plates from the buffet.

Finally, it came time to talk about the price tag which meant it was Astrid's turn to take over the conversation. She reviewed the requirements and timeline which had been presented and concluded that the ships would need to be in place within five weeks. She then handed a sheet of paper to Giulia which contained the EU's cost and pricing estimates on it for six and 12 months.

Giulia raised her eyebrows, put the paper down and said "We're not talking about renting paddle boats here. These are serious capabilities to counter the threat you described."

Realizing they had miscalculated, Astrid quickly said "This is just a starting point for us, but we really need to know what kind of price you had in mind."

Without hesitating, Giulia responded, "Twelve billion euros for each six months, plus ammunition costs and fully insuring any damage to our fleet."

Everyone else in the room gasped. Alex's face went pale.

Giulia continued, "You are asking us to risk our fleet and personnel against two powerful states who may also punish us elsewhere for taking sides against them during a crisis."

Astrid motioned to someone at the door who quickly went outside to make a phone call to Wouters.

"But that is an enormous sum of money. It's so much more than you charged us for your work in the Red Sea" Max said.

"Max, my friend, the Houthis were dangerous, but their reach was also very limited. Asking us to help you against Russia and Turkey means we could lose our whole Argonaut Marine fleet, and perhaps other vessels from the Argonaut fleet as punishment. So, the risk and the cost are connected," Giulia responded.

"If anything, my boss may even be angry I did not ask for even more" Giulia said. She was clearly playing the negotiating game well and Astrid quickly realized they were outmatched.

"OK, so let's take another break and eat something, Astrid said.

About 25 minutes later the break was still going on when Wouters and another EU official appeared at the door and motioned Astrid to step outside. Giulia knew what this meant and allowed herself to smile, but not too much. The truth was that Argonaut Marine did not really need to take this risk, but this was also why Basil built the fleet - to put himself in a position to gain no matter the situation.

After the break, Wouters and the other EU official joined the discussion which led to a back and forth with Giulia over costs, timing, and command arrangements. The longer they talked, the more it became clear that Cyprus and the EU really had few options other than Argonaut Marine.

At one point Wouters asked Giulia, "Are you sure this is your lowest price?"

Giulia paused for a moment, then responded, "Every time I read about the value of these gas fields in Cyprus they are quoted as valued at 20-40 billion Euros, and how many are there?"

"14 right now" Alex responded.

Giulia went on, "So they are worth somewhere between 280-560 billion euros, which makes us a very reasonable insurance policy to have."

Finally, Wouters concluded, "OK, so let's work together to refine the terms and conditions on both sides because this will require a decision of the European Council"

"Very well," Giulia said. "I will have our legal and finance team get in contact through Max and Astrid tonight, then you can direct them to their right people in your offices."

They all nodded in agreement.

Giulia thanked them for lunch as they all shook hands. She then retrieved her phone from the box and walked out, her heels clicking on the floor the only sound to be heard in a room left in stunned silence.

Alex had a quick chat with Astrid, Max, Klara, and Pawel before leaving and heading over to the Cyprus Mission to the EU, where Ambassador Costas was waiting to hear how the first negotiations went. He knew already it would be a long night since the ambassador would want to call the foreign minister and maybe even the president that night and Alex would need to be there since he was in the room that day.

Alex had lost track of time but finally got back to his hotel and made a video call to Marietta and he was hoping to say goodnight to his children. But the one-hour time zone difference meant he missed their bedtime.

"You look like a wreck," Marietta said.

"Do I?" He asked. "Well, you always said you did not marry me for my looks."

That night Giulia was already on her flight back to Dubai but not before sending a coded text message to Basil using the Signal app on her phone. "Main course and desert," was all it said.

## Moscow

The Russian Special Communications and Information Service had long been able to intercept telephone calls in Cyprus, to watch Russian oligarchs hiding money from Moscow and to keep an eye on the British airbase there. But a careless phone call from a Cypriot foreign ministry official to his daughter, asking her forgiveness since he would miss her ballet recital that evening revealed much. And when he blamed "the Turks and Russians" to his daughter, it told the Kremlin their plans to seize the gas platforms would need to be accelerated.

They also received reporting from their assets in Brussels that Giulia Rovigo, the director of Argonaut marine had been seen in Brussels. The Center did not believe it was a coincidence so a plan to deal with this company had to be formulated quickly.

## Nicosia

Alex arrived home bleary eyed and exhausted. He could not sleep all night as he ran through every possible scenario in his mind. "What if there is no consensus at the EU? Would we be left on our own? Who would pay for Argonaut Marine? What future is there for Cyprus without her energy resources?"

Alex briefed the national security council that afternoon on his meetings in Brussels, having already updated the president the night before. He also advised the president that it was time to reach out to the Egyptians and Israelis since the EU may not be able to field a large enough force to keep the Turks and Russians out – especially without Argonaut Marine. If Cyprus had to pay for Giulia's fleet by itself, what could be the price?

Eleni nodded and said "Thanks Alex, I've already started talks with Cairo and Jerusalem.

The MOD spoke next and discussed their coordination with the navies of France, Greece, Italy, Spain, Croatia, and others for a maritime "exercise" to be conducted starting within 3-4 weeks. The minister made it clear that with or without any additional help, they would do their duty and defend Cyprus the best they could.

### Brussels

The European Council worked feverishly in the days since Wouters and the other staff members met with Argonaut Marine at their discreet rendezvous in Uccle. The Council Secretariat faced a complex task, how to arrange for discussions to enable fast decisions on a series issues. First was to decide on a request from Cyprus to simultaneously declare Article 42(7) and Article 222. Next was a decision to establish an EU maritime mission to prevent the potential seizure of energy platforms in Cyprus' exclusive economic zone, the EU's main internal energy supply.

Finally, a decision was required for the EU to pay Argonaut Marine to augment its effort in the eastern Mediterranean. Cyprus needed all three decisions to be a yes to have a chance to maintain its sovereignty and keep its many gas fields in EU hands. Another decision about economic sanctions on Turkey and Russia would be held off until an actual shooting war started.

They also could not declare Article 42 (7) until a member state had been attacked. So, this decision was also set aside for consideration later as the need arose.

The following week, all three decisions were set to be decided but the order of them was changed. It made no sense to approve an EU military mission without Argonaut Marine, since it would probably not deter the Russians and Turks and lead the EU into a shooting war – with Europe at a disadvantage from the start.

Instead, the first decision was to activate the EU's Solidarity Clause under Article 222 to allow various EU entities to fund and support various activities in support of Cyprus. It passed the European Council with a unanimous vote on Tuesday.

By now, news of these deliberations had leaked into the media in Brussels. Given how leaky the European institutions were already, it was a miracle it had not leaked earlier. This news led to a global spike in natural gas prices, reaching a five-year high by the end of Wednesday. Moscow and Ankara denied they had any such plans while military bloggers started to speculate and share indicators of Russian activity gleaned from open sources. Some of it was accurate but much of it was not.

That same day, the deliberations on funding Argonaut Marine were tied together with the decision to establish an EU military mission in the Eastern Mediterranean. It would all come down to this day.

Within the stuffy European Council room at Justus Lipsus, Astrid and Max sat on the second row of seats and sweated through their clothes as the day went on. The discussions seemed promising at first but the Hungarians and Slovakians were sour on the idea. Numerous breaks were taken so the chair, along with France, Germany, and the Lithuanian presidency could work on the Hungary and Slovakia to bring them into the consensus. They offered several incentives but neither one budged. At the end of the last break, the French ambassador looked toward Ambassador Costas and closed his eyes with a combination of anger and sadness.

When the vote finally came, both Hungary and Slovakia voted no and thus ended any hope of an EU force to protect Cyprus plus any funding for Argonaut Marine.

Astrid ran from the room to grab her phone and text Alex. Everyone sneered at the Slovakian and Hungarian ambassadors as they left the room. One person standing along the wall coughed the word "Vatnik" as they walked past.

The French and Cypriot ambassadors conferred in the corner and were soon joined by several other ambassadors.

About 20 minutes later, the group of ambassadors stood before the press downstairs and announced that a coalition of the willing was being established to provide maritime and air forces to protect Cyprus. The French would lead the coalition and they would work alongside Cyprus to access EU funding through the Solidarity Clause to help defray costs.

In private, they also discussed how this new coalition could come up with the money to pay for Argonaut Marine to support their effort. While some spoke in public how ready they were to support Cyprus, even fewer were ready to commit forces to what looked increasingly to be the losing side.

And even fewer were willing to open their checkbooks to pay for a private military company for what could be an indefinite time period. Eight billion euros plus their own operating costs every six months could quickly eat up their defense budgets, especially when they still shoring up defenses against an increasingly aggressive Russia in eastern and central Europe. Momentum was everything and right now, it was not on their side. In the end, most of the funding would need to come from Cyprus itself.

### Dubai

Giulia received a call that night from Max, telling her the vote had failed but that they were still looking for ways to find the money. She half expected this kind of outcome already and so did her boss Basil when she told him not ten minutes after Max's call. But Basil seemed almost giddy at the news.

"Perfect," he said.

"Really?" Giulia responded.

"Yes, my dear" Basil said. "This could be the best outcome so far."

"But why?" Giulia asked.

"Because it could give us an even bigger payoff," he said.

Giulia seemed puzzled, "OK, but how?"

"You'll see," Basil replied. "Meet me in Cairo in two days and invite your new friends from Nicosia."

"I see," Giulia replied. "We'll send the details to Fiona" Basil's executive assistant.

"Very well, see you soon" Basil said, and he hung up.

### Nicosia

Alex wondered if Marietta would ever forgive him for being so tired and stressed out. He let his temper get the better of him that night at dinner when Stavros was acting out and Klio decided to join in. For most Cypriot men, acting out this way was quite normal, but Marietta would not stand for it. She was a psychotherapist and was constantly harping on Alex that they not pass along their own trauma and bad habits to their kids. "We must be the ones to end the cycle" she was constantly reminding him. So, on this night, she asked him to leave the table.

The cabinet meeting that day had been a tense mess as the foreign minister reported that Israel needed more convincing and Egypt would like to help, but if there was such a threat coming to the region, they preferred to prioritize their own energy infrastructure.

Just when Alex did not think his day could get any worse, he received a call from the president's office to pack his bags for travel to Cairo tomorrow. He would be joined by Eleni, the energy minister, and an official from the finance ministry.

He only had one clean work shirt left so he washed two more that night and hoped no one would see the wrinkles because there would be no time to iron them. He told Marietta he had to leave again the next morning and her anger at him only got worse. He hated that he would leave without them having made up.

The next morning, he woke up at 6am and crept downstairs to shower and get ready for an early flight. When he emerged from the bathroom Marietta was standing waiting for him.

She hugged him closely and whispered "I can't imagine the stress you are under. Please know that I love you and believe in you."

They hugged and swayed for a few minutes, then she made him breakfast. They kissed at the door, and he was off before the children were awake.

### Four Seasons Hotel, Cairo

Basil Kostatakis woke up early in the ambassador suite and opened the curtains to seethe early morning sun on the Nile. People who have not been to Cairo often don't realize how lush and green the city can be along the river.

The pilot and crew of his Grumman Gulfstream were staying a few floors below along with Giulia and his attorney Roger Applethwaite, an old classmate and friend from Cambridge. Basil's own security team was staying in the rooms adjacent to him, supported by the Egyptian police. It was one of the many benefits of his arrangement with Cairo.

Giulia rang him around 9am to let him know the Cypriots had arrived and were ready to see him at lunchtime upstairs. She still was not sure of Basil's plans for this meeting and assumed he would try to extend a line of credit to the Cypriots so they could rent his fleet.

Eleni, Alex, the energy minister, and a lawyer from the Cypriot ministry of justice made their way to the rooftop restaurant and found it empty. A hostess showed them to an oval shaped table by a window overlooking the Nile. About 10 minutes later, Basil, Giulia, and Roger showed up. They all exchanged handshakes and business cards while an aperitif was served before sitting down together. Lunch was served as they began to nibble on their salads and marvel at the view before Basil broke the ice.

"So, I understand you need our help," Basil said.

Eleni responded, "So it seems. That is why we came here."

"And the EU can't help you?" Basil asked.

They can, but we need more help than they can provide" she said.

Basil nodded and said, "Very well, I'll let Roger explain our offer."

Roger sat up and spoke, "So as we understand it, your needs may go way beyond just 6-12 months since those other parties will not just disappear. We think you need a lasting solution, and our offer will deliver just that."

"OK, what is the offer?" Eleni asked.

Roger looked quickly at Giulia before responding, then answered, "We can offer you the protection of our fleet whenever needed in exchange for the following."

Eleni and Alex took in a deep breath.

Roger continued. "We'll need full basing rights in Cyprus and since you've not yet awarded Block 14 to anyone, we want a 99 year lease on it for one euro."

The Cypriots' eyes opened wide.

"Oh, and we don't want to pay any taxes. We'll pay our share of gas revenues to you like the others for anything we extract, but charging taxes is a bit much when we'll be protecting you," Roger concluded.

After letting it sink in for a moment, Basil asked, "So, what do you say?"

Eleni and Alex looked at each other and the Energy Ministry rep looked crestfallen. Then, Eleni spoke up.

"This is quite a high price Mr. Kostatakis. Block 14 is estimated to be worth 40 billion euros so, it seems your price has gone way up since last week," Eleni said.

Basil nodded and spoke. "What value are any of these gas fields to you if Turkey and Russia control them? You'd lose everything; your economic future and being surrounded by unfriendly neighbors. This solution gives you the best chance for a bright future."

The Cypriots felt the vise starting to squeeze them. *"What choice do we have?"* Alex thought.

Eleni replied, "As you know, we've already lost so much territory, including so many of our family homes, and we live under constant threat of losing more. I will need to contact our president before I can give you any kind of answer."

"I understand," Basil replied. "Shall we meet again for lunch here tomorrow to discuss it?"

"Yes," Eleni replied. "We should have some kind of answer by then."

She then stood up which told the rest of the Cypriot delegation to do the same. They shook hands with their hosts and left their lunch uneaten on the table.

Eleni, Alex, and the rest of their group took the elevator downstairs and boarded a taxi heading for Cyprus' embassy which was 15 minutes away. There they could speak to their president and cabinet using secure means. These matters were too sensitive to speak over a mobile phone, even on the most secure applications.

### Port Said, Egypt

That afternoon, Basil and Giulia took a helicopter up to their base in Port Said to check on the fleet and discuss how they could run this new mission if Nicosia agreed. Roger stayed behind with an assistant to work on the contracts they would place in front of the Cypriots the next day.

Once Basil and Giulia landed at the Port Said airport, there was a large black van waiting for them next to their own company limousine and security team on the tarmac.

Before disembarking the helicopter, Basil called his security details on the radio to ask who was in the van. He responded, "They are some men who want to talk business with you."

"Hmm, OK." Basil said.

Giulia grabbed the microphone and said, "But tell them we'll only speak with them inside our vehicle, and I want the security team to make their driver wait outside the car and check him for weapons.

I want your eyes open and send for the standby team now just in case. Once they are here on the tarmac, we can proceed."

"OK, we're on it," the security chief.

About 15 minutes later, Basil and Giulia stepped off the helicopter and into the Argonaut Marine limousine. About five minutes later, two men stepped into the limousine after being frisked by Basil's security detail.

"Good afternoon, Mister Kostatakis, I am Maxim Plekhanov, of the Wagner Group. This is my friend Mehmet Demir from the company SADORA. We have a proposal for you from some friends of ours."

Giulia's shifted in her seat and started to look perturbed.

"OK, I'm listening," Basil said.

Giulia shot Basil a glare.

Plekhanov proceeded to speak, "We understand there are certain people in Europe who wish to hire your services and we would also like a chance to make a bid."

"I'm not sure you need my help for what you're planning, do you?" Basil responded.

"Not exactly, Plekhanov said. "We are willing to pay you to do nothing."

"OK, but then how much?" Basil asked.

"We can match their offer or better. Say 10 billion euros. Plus, then you won't need to fight against us," Plekhanov said.

"Everybody wins," Mehmet added.

"So that's it?" Basil asked.

"I'm not sure what you mean" Plekhanov replied.

"Can you offer me something juicier, like perhaps gas rights?" Basil said.

"Is that what they offered you?" Mehmet asked.

Basil nodded. Giulia's looked perplexed since she knew this was a lie.

Plekhanov and Mehmet looked at each other.

"We were prepared for this," Plekhanov said. "So, we can offer you 10 billion euros, plus the gas rights for the unassigned Block 14 and you won't have to fight us. What do you say?"

Ever pushing the envelope, Basil wanted to press for more.

"What about basing rights? I'd like guaranteed passage into the Black Sea and port rights in Tartus," referring to the Russian naval base in Syria.

The Russian replied, we can discuss those details later.

"And you'll leave Egyptian interests alone? You know we already have a close relationship with them." Basil asked.

"Of course," Plekhanov said. "We are still working to rebuild our fraternal relations here so no need to worry about that."

Basil did not notice but Giulia's face had gone stone cold.

"Well gentlemen, give me your contact information and let's speak again tomorrow night. Now we have some important work to do and hanging around here prevents us from doing that," Basil said.

They handed their business cards to Giulia and left the car.

Basil turned to Giulia and said, "Not bad, and we win either way." He then let a smirk come to his face while she stared out the window and did not respond. They headed to Port Said for the bulk of the afternoon before flying back to Cairo later that day.

Once they entered the hotel lobby, Basil invited Giulia to dinner that night to which she agreed. They would meet in the lobby at eight o'clock.

She promptly went to her room and took a long shower. She felt dirty after what she had witnessed on the tarmac, and she could not seem to clean it off her. She then packed her bag and had a courier move it to another nearby hotel. She then pulled out Alex's card to make sure she had it, along with the cards of the Russian and Turkish gentlemen who surprised them on the tarmac.

At 8pm Giulia walked into the lobby of the Four Seasons wearing a black jumpsuit and with her hair in a tight braid. She looked ready for a fight.

As soon as Basil arrived downstairs, he greeted her and pointed toward a car that was waiting to take them to dinner.

"No evening gown I see," Basil remarked.

She glared at him and said, "I can't believe you are even considering that offer from the Russians and Turks."

Looking slightly amused, Basil replied "My dear, I must do what is best for the company. How else do you think I've grown my business?"

"Fuck you, I'm not your dear," Giulia spat out. "I did not sign up for this shit."

"Well of course you did,' he replied. "You knew what you were getting into." He continued, "Look, now we can negotiate an even better deal from the Cypriots and if not, we take the deal from the Russians. This deal could give us the capital to finally expand into east Asia."

"I can't believe you, going against Europe to fill your pockets even more. I thought you were honorable, but now I see the truth," she said.

"So, dinner then?" he asked and motioned toward the waiting car.

"No, not now – not ever." Giulia said. She then turned on her heel and walked out of the hotel.

A stunned Basil was left speechless. He was not used to anyone saying no to him.

**Embassy of Cyprus, Cairo**

Eleni, Alex, and the team just finished a long and solemn video teleconference with the president and cabinet. It pained them to be extorted into giving up lucrative gas rights in Block 14 to a bandit who may not keep his promise to protect them or keep changing the terms of any agreement.

Eleni also realized just how deep Egypt's relationship with Argonaut Marine had gone. During a recent phone call with her counterpart at the foreign ministry in Cairo apologized, they could not do much since they were also concerned about their own energy platforms.

That left only the Israel card to play. If she could get Israel to support Cyprus in this crisis, then the Americans would also be onboard. While both were radioactive in the region after the invasion of Gaza and Lebanon, it could just work. It was a dangerous game, but she had little choice.

Her conversations the past few days with Israeli deputy foreign minister Avi had leaned in a positive direction, they still were not ready to commit – citing the same concerns that Egypt had. Avi was an old friend with whom she had stayed in close contact for years, so she knew she he would be open to if she could bring more to the table.

Upon leaving the embassy, Alex retrieved his phone from the secure box and found three missed phone calls from an unknown number. He also found a text message on the Signal app from Giulia, telling him to text her as soon as possible.

"Hi, what can I do for you?" he texted.

Giulia replied immediately, "I need to see you asap. Meet me at the restaurant Porta D'Oro in one hour. Come alone"

Alex turned to Eleni and the others he would catch up to them later. He then pulled Eleni aside and told her what was happening and to please stay up just in case there was a new twist in the negotiation. Eleni was annoyed that she had not been the one contacted but had to trust that Alex knew what he was doing.

"Just don't give anything away and not a word about what we are considering," she admonished.

"Of course, minister, Alex replied.

He then took a tax back down to central Cairo.

### Porta D'Oro, Cairo

Alex found Giulia sitting in a table in the very back of the rustic Italian restaurant. He was mostly happy to finally have a chance to eat since lunch had been cut short and they'd spent hours in the embassy with only crackers to nibble on. Giulia was already eating crostini and she offered him to take from the plate. He felt almost rude as he devoured three of them before ordering a full meal once the waiter came around.

"I'm glad you could come," Giulia said.

"Yeah, thanks, Alex replied as he took off his tie and shoved it into his briefcase.

"That was really something today," Alex said.

"You have no idea," Giulia replied as she shook her head.

"I mean, what is it like working for that guy?" Alex asked.

"I can't really say since I quit tonight," Giulia shared.

"What? Really?" Alex responded as he pushed back from the table.

"Si" she said as the food arrived.

"No wait, you just quit. Why?" Alex asked,then tucked into a bowl of pasta.

"It's a long story but in the end, I need to be able to live with myself," Giulia said.

"You mean the way he was squeezing us for a natural gas field?" Alex said.

"Partially, but mostly because the Russians and Turks also made an offer to us today. I would have told them to fuck off, but he is actually considering it," Giulia answered.

"My God, are you serious?" Alex asked, incredulous.

"Absolutely," Giulia responded and placed the business cards of the Russian and Turkish representatives on the table. "I'm not kidding," she said.

"Take a good picture of them," Giulia instructed Alex. He did so immediately and texted them to Eleni with a note "will explain later."

"OK, so what else?" Alex asked.

"They offered to give Basil the same gas field after they take it plus ten billion euros," Giulia stated. "In his mind, he wins either way" she added.

"And you could not go along with that?" Alex inquired.

"Absolutely not!" Giulia almost shouted. "I can't look my old colleagues in the eye or even myself in the mirror if I was part of such a thing. The shame would kill me," she said.

"I would rather starve with integrity than feast on immorality" Giulia added.

"What will you do now?" Alex asked.

"I have already made more money than I could imagine, plus I have my navy pension, so I should be just fine," she answered. "My grandparents left me an old house in Belluno so maybe I can fix it up and enjoy life there" she added.

"That sounds like a dream," Alex said.

Their conversation continued for another 45 minutes while Alex picked at his plate and Giulia gave him more details to help Cyprus navigate its way through this crisis. He also talked about Marietta and his kids and how much he could not wait to see them again after so many nights at work and on the road.

"Maybe someday I can do some consulting for you if I feel like leaving the mountains" she joked.

"But seriously, if you go to the negotiations again tomorrow, be ready for him to ask for even more since now he has his bidding war. It's like a casino, the house always wins," she said.

"OK, thanks. I will pay for the dinner since you are unemployed now. It's the least I can do," Alex said.

"Grazie Alex," Giulia replied and chuckled.

"But seriously, thank you so much. You have no idea what this means for us" Alex said. "You will always be welcome in Cyprus."

With that she left for her new hotel. Instead of staying another night in Cairo, she booked a flight to Rome that left at midnight. She wanted to make sure her old Italian navy mentors knew what she decided and why before taking a train to Belluno.

### Hilton Cairo

Alex walked fast into the lobby and took the elevator to the seventh floor where Eleni was waiting in room 704. Once inside, he found the energy minister and finance ministry representative already there wearing t-shirts and sweatpants.

Alex told them everything that Giulia had shared with him and showed them the photo of the Russian and Turkish representative's business cards, which Eleni had already sent to Nicosia.

They considered all the options for how they can make the best use of this information. Israel's interests certainly would not be served if Turkey and Russia took control of Cyprus' gas platforms, and now that had the smoking gun to prove it. And since they were now on the verge of co-opting Argonaut Marine in the process, what if they hired the company to help seize Israel's platforms as well? But was that enough to get Jerusalem to stand in solidarity with Cyprus?

The energy minister finally said what he had been avoiding saying so far.

"There is already an Israeli company bidding on Block 14 so why don't we give it to them to sweeten the deal? Maybe even give them special terms?" he said.

"That's it!" Eleni shouted. "Can we just do that?" she asked.

"As energy minister, I set the rules so while it may cause some other companies to get angry, it's something I already have the authority to decide" he said.

Alex spoke up, "Israel may not have a big navy, but their air force is the most powerful in the Middle East, plus they have nuclear weapons. That could change the equation for the Turks and Russians."

Eleni nodded and added, "Also if Israel is in trouble, it could bring the Americans back. They wouldn't let their little brother face Russia and Turkey alone. It's got to work."

Eleni looked at Alex and said, "You must go back home since the president will need you there for these next steps." She hugged and thanked him for his vital role that night, then he left to go pack and sleep for an early morning flight. She then checked her watch to see if it was too late to call anyone.

### Jerusalem, Israel

The next day Eleni arrived at Ben Gurion Airport and ignored the messages from Basil's assistant asking why she had not yet shown up to their second meeting as planned.

That afternoon Eleni and the energy minister arrived at the Israeli foreign ministry in Givat Ram neighborhood of Jerusalem. She was also accompanied by a senior Cypriot MOD official and the deputy director of KYP.

Her old friend Avi Glickman, the deputy foreign minister and a group of officials from various ministries greeted them and they all sat down. Once the formalities were completed, Eleni spoke.

"Avi, Have I got a deal for you."

### Nicosia

Alex arrived home dead tired that morning, thankful that the flight had only been an hour long. Marietta greeted him at the door and had a late breakfast waiting for him. He did not even bother to open his suitcase or put anything away. The president would not need him until that night, so he did not bother to go into the office.

He took a shower, then laid on the bed, finally able to rest. Marietta sat on the bed next to him and reminded him the children would not be home from school for at least another few hours, so they had the place all to themselves.

"Maybe you can just take a nap" she said.

When she turned to look at him, he was already asleep.

### Brussels

A few days later Wouters had a long visit from Ambassador Costas, who relayed to him what happened in Cairo. Once Costas left, Wouters closed his door again and made several telephone calls.

45 minutes later he came to Astrid's office and said, "Come with me and be ready to take notes. We are going to the High Representative's Office."

Astrid asked, "What is happening?"

Wouters turned and said, "The game has changed. There is a rabid dog that needs to be put down."

# CHAPTER THREE

# THE REST OF YOUR LIFE

Carl was in no rush to lace up his boots, doing it methodically as he pondered the day ahead. It seemed silly that he had to do these things here, but he no longer wondered. It made him feel a little more normal.

He walked to the console and clocked in, starting his shift. It was ironic since shifts never truly ended. A few more months of working in this dreary place and he'd be out of debt.

He quickly solved some easy problems with his AI partner, then video called his daughter Irene, or at least her avatar. At least they got her deep brown eyes right. She said his mother Daphne was very sick and everyone wanted him to visit before she died.

He felt shocked but not surprised since this was exactly the kind of thing he feared when he took this job. He told Irene he would try to get back as soon as possible and to let him know if anything changes. She asked if he would he still come back if his mother died before he could see her one last time? That was a question he did not know how to answer.

"Let's just focus on seeing her while she's still breathing" he said.

"OK Dad. I love you." Irene curtly replied, then her avatar disappeared.

He worked on a few more difficult tasks for an hour. Then he called his advanced AI supervisor Pegasus 3. Carl explained the situation and asked to take time off to see his ailing mother one last time before she dies. P3 (as Carl referred to his boss) acted confused.

"Why can't she visit you here in the metaverse?" The AI asked, its voice sounding almost human.

"She's too old and frail for that." Carl explained.

"I see," responded P3. "We might have a way for you to visit her, but any time away will have to be repaid. As per your employment contract, it is an extra three months added to your work term for every week you are away."

Carl was shocked. "But I have only six months left in here, isn't there some other way?" he pleaded.

"This was all in your contract," P3 said sounding confused as to how Carl might not remember the details of the 300 plus page document he had signed a year and a half earlier. "Any time off is very costly for Biosmart. You must be removed from the network, only to later be plugged back in. This requires many resources."

Carl, now begging, said "Please, this is my mother we're talking about."

P3 responded "I gave you an option and it's the only one. But if this impacts your work and your performance drops below the line, your time won't count anyway."

A defeated Carl replied "Thank you for giving me this option, I'll take it. I am most grateful."

"Very well, at the end of your shift we'll start the exit protocol." P3 responded then left his view.

A few hours later, Carl had to meet with the HR AI. He electronically signed a document agreeing to work six more months. In return, he would get two weeks off to see his sick mother.

"OK, that should do it for now. Also please remember that if you run out on your debt, we can find you and plug you back in without pay." The HR AI robot said in a soft voice that sounded flat but foreboding.

"Yes, I understand" he sullenly replied.

**Biosmart Facility**
**Vallejo, California**

The technicians arrived at Carl's pod after pushing a gurney cart across the cavernous structure. Inside were well almost two-hundred pods full of AI brainworkers. This Vallejo location was almost full, and a new one is being built near Pittsburgh. Another one is also planned in a suburb of Tulsa.

Wearing a biosuit to ensure no contaminants nor viruses can affect the workers suspended in the pods, one technician pushed a series of buttons to unplug Carl's pod from the AI and start his removal process. First, they attached a sedative to his IV and reached in to remove the breathing mask and feeding tube.

The technicians saw Carl was breathing normally and then began draining the gel substance he was suspended in. This gel prevented bed sores and absorbed waste from his body. It was was constantly circulated in and out of the pod to remove waste and impurities and keep his skin moist and healthy. Afterwards, the electrodes that were connected to his body to prevent muscle atrophy were taken off one by one.

Before proceeding, they rechecked his vital signs then slowly removed the brain-computer interface cables from his implants. Once he was completely unplugged and ready, he was moved onto the gurney and covered with a mylar blanket. He was then taken into the medical facility where we was washed and placed into a private recovery room to recuperate. The company maintained a policy that never allowed brainworkers, nor anyone else, to see where their bodies were stored while they were working.

Eventually, Carl woke and opened his eyes. Everything was blurry, painful, and he was hungry. He let out a groan.

"Take it easy," the nurse tech said.

"When can I eat and then leave here?" he asked.

"Normally it takes two days after being unplugged before you'll be ready to safely leave here. Oh, and your lunch will be here any minute now" they replied.

"Oh crap, two of my 14 days already?" he murmured. "Nobody told me that."

"Just rest and after you eat someone will be by to work with you to get your range of motion back," they replied and left.

He checked out his body the best he could since lying still for over a year left him stiff and sore. He felt his stomach and it felt slimmer. So at least he lost some belly fat. *They should advertise weight loss when they sell people on this work*, he thought.

His hair had grown longer too, something else to take care of before he saw his mother since she always remarked on his appearance.

He touched the implants on his body, his hand lingering on the one behind his right ear. It connected him to the metaverse workspace, where he had been for the past 14 months.

*I'm going to look like a freak*, he thought as he imagined seeing everyone again in two days. *Maybe it's best to leave my hair this way*, he pondered, *so no one can see his one visible implant.*

A cheerful assistant came soon after to help him move his joints and take his first steps in over 400 days.

"I thought I would get to eat first!" he protested to no avail.

She lifted his arms and legs, moving them gently. Then she asked him to wiggle his fingers and toes. She sat him up and he felt the warm sunlight through the window. His eyes felt like they were burning.

The assistant stepped over and handed him a pair of sun goggles "You'd better put these on. After your eyes being closed for so long, they'll need time to adjust."He put them on and stared out the window.

It was then that Carl became aware of smell again, which felt odd and wonderful at the same time. Even though the place had a scrubbed sterile smell to it, the sudden smell of food was exhilarating.

A tech walked in with a tray. "You must be starving," they said. Ravenous, Carl ate the bland food with gusto and drank everything they put in front of him.

The assistant led him on a walk through some hallways. He took slow steps and almost fell a few times. The longer he walked, the more he tired out but also the more confident he felt walking again.

He could not wait to eat again and spent the day eating, walking, and watching TV. Had TV always been this bad or did it get worse while he was gone? Then, he decided that he did not miss TV, so he chose to take a walk outside if that was allowed.

He stood outside in the cool October air of Vallejo. He felt the wind and saw the tall fence around the building and remembered noticing it when he first came here to pay off his debts.

The next day he called his brother Tim to arrange to pick him up that evening. Tim arrived around six in the evening as the sun was setting and he met him at the gate after getting back his belongings and clothes in a what felt like a movie scene of someone being let out of a prison.

His clothes fit loosely on him since he had lost weight and when Tim gave him a big hug, he did not feel enough strength to hug him back with the same energy.

"Got weak in there eh?" Tim chortled. "Man, I'm happy to see you!"

"Yeah, thanks. It feels so good to be out herein the world again. How is Mom?" He replied.

Looking away, Tim replied "Mom is fading fast, and I hope she can see you before it's all over. "

"Let's go straight to the hospital then." He spoke.

Tim nodded and said, "That's what I was thinking."

They got into the car and start the hour-long drive to Santa Rosa.

"I'm so glad they let you come out to see Mom" Tim said.

"Yeah, me too but it's going to cost me another six months in there." he said solemnly.

Tim jerked in his seat "Oh man, that's terrible. Don't they have any hearts?"

Carl responded, "Of course not, they're mostly just machines."

Tim let out a sigh "I wish you weren't doing all of this."

"All of what?" he quickly said.

"This" Tim spat out. "Being put under and plugged into a machine for almost two years."

Closing his eyes in frustration, he replied "Look Tim, we've been through this so many times. This was the only way."

"The only way, are you so sure?"

Carl was frustrated. He said, "Once we inherited Dad's medical debt and then Giselle got sick, there was no other way to pay it off. And I am not leaving any debt to Irene and Marco, so I had to do this."

"Yeah, I know bro, but this is brutal. Ever since they changed the laws, everyone is inheriting debt instead of houses or money. And people can't go bankrupt anymore, only companies can. It's so fucked up" Tim said.

"Tell me about it" Carl deadpanned.

"So, what exactly do they have you do in there?" Tim asked.

Carl explained that artificial intelligence performs more effectively when paired with a human brain. As a result, they created a company that pays people big money to be that brain. "So, I help the AI to solve problems, research things, and so on. Some days it's overwhelming how much I learn and see."

Tim smiled and said, "No offense bro, but you were never a rocket scientist or anything."

Carl laughed "I know, but it doesn't need to be a brilliant mind to do the trick, just a human one."

"What about the other people there, are they all like you?" Tim asked.

Carl replied "I have no idea, its not like you're allowed to hang out together, even when you are inside of the metaverse. I think most are people like me, they have big debts, or they inherited them, and this is one sure way to pay it off. But during my off time, I do get to hang out with other people who come in there for fun."

"Oh yeah, any hot ladies?" Tim asked impishly.

Carl was silent for a moment then said, "C'mon bro, after Giselle I still feel like a zombie."

"Sorry man, she was the greatest." Tim said.

"Yeah, she was" Carl replied "And thanks for looking after Marco and Irene while I've been under. I can't wait to see them."

"Of course, brother!" Tim boomed "And they are doing great. Irene is trying to take on the mom role and Marco is not always OK with that but otherwise they are normal kids in their 20s."

"Yeah, I don't know how I can do this for an extra six months." Carl said "Being away so long and not being able to see them in real life really tears me up. Irene visits me with her avatar sometimes, but Marco still seems mad at me for going away and doing this."

Tim held the wheel with one hand and turned to his brother saying "Someday he will understand what you are doing for him and be grateful. I mean, I can't imagine all the things he'll be able to do starting his adult life without all that debt hanging over his head."

Carl raised his voice "Dude, watch the road! Yeah, I don't want them to live like we've had to. It's bad enough losing their mother but to inherit two generations of medical debt is just too much."

"Right on bro, and that is love right there. You are a great father" Tim said.

Carl took a deep breath and replied, "Thanks brother."

They drove the rest of the way mostly in silence while an oldies radio station hosted a tribute Jackson Browne, playing "Running on Empty" as they rounded the San Pablo Bay.

**Saint Joseph's Hospital**
**Santa Rosa**

Tim's Nissan SUV pulled into the parking lot, and he turned to him "You ready for this?" He nodded and they got out of the car and went inside to the oncology ward.

Once they arrived at their mother's room, Irene came running over crying and hugged her father. "She's gone" she sobbed. "About 20 minutes ago."

Crestfallen, Carl's shoulders slumped as he hugged his daughter tightly then rushed into the room to see a nurse packing up an IV pump and rolling it away. There on the bed his mother laid, looking frail and at peace.

Tearing up, he placed his hand on her cold forehead and touched her hand saying, "I'm so sorry Mom, I got here as soon as I could."

Tim and Irene hugged him as they all sobbed and sniffled.

Carl then asked "Where is Marco? Does he know?"

"Yes Dad, I texted him just before you go here" Irene replied.

A while later Marco arrived after driving up from Salinas. Carl, Tim, and Irene resisted the nurses taking her body so Marco and some of her grandchildren could say goodbye. One by one they arrived and cried as they said their farewells to Grandma Daphne

They held the funeral in Santa Rosa four days later, or rather her Celebration of Life as they called it. Carl's two sisters, Holly and Christina, were also there with their families. Many cousins and friends that Carl hadn't seen in along time were also present. The thought of having to go back to Biosmart and be put under for another year caused him to feel painful emotions.

That evening, a chimenea was set up on Tim's deck. Around a dozen people sat on chairs, sipping drinks and socializing by the warm fire.

"You don't have to go back there" whispered someone into Carl's ear as the fire crackled in the background.

"What do you mean?" Carl replied as he turned to look at his son-in-law Matt, Irene's husband.

"There is a way for you to escape and never have to go back there" Matt said.

Incredulous, Carl responded "But how? These implants are like having tracking devices installed in my body – they'd find me and put me back in there, possibly for good."

"I know some people who can take them out and let you escape. It's a group of activists and doctors and they know what they are doing." Matt whispered.

"I'd love to believe you but what then? What about the debt? I don't want to live the rest of my life on the run." Carl said as his voice went from a whisper to a more normal tone.

"Shh, let's go out front and talk" Matt whispered.

Matt and Carl left the circle on the deck and walked around toward the front of the house, stopping in the side yard, out of earshot from the group.

Matt then started to speak "First off, those places assume all your debt when you sign up with them to work it off so there is no legal way it could fall onto Irene and Marco."

"OK, I remember that much. But what about these implants? They told me only Biosmart can remove them without me possibly having severe brain damage." Carl said.

"They have a surgeon on the team and so they can usually take them out with no harm."Matt responded.

Carl stammered "Usually?"

Matt replied "Yes, usually they can take them out with no brain damage, but the ones they can't are disabled so they can't hurt you and can't track you."

"So, I could be stuck with these forever?" Carl sighed.

Seeking to assuage Carl's anguish, Matt replied, "Yes...maybe, but you'd also be free."

"And who are these activists? How do I know they can be trusted?" Carl asked.

Matt explained, "They are mostly people who used to work in the industry but who got disillusioned when they saw how it was being used. Did you know that almost no one who signs up for Biosmart only serves the original contract? They always find ways to tack on more debt or more time so you can never completely leave."

"Oh jeez, so it's like a prison." Carl said.

"Or serfdom," Matt added.

"Fuck me." Carl exhaled and put his hand on his forehead. After a few minutes of silence, he looked back at Matt and said, "OK, what's the plan?"

### Lake Tahoe

The next day he was packed up in Tim's Nissan and heading up to Lake Tahoe with Matt for a "planned family gathering." Irene and Marco would meet them up there.

"So, you were in on this too?" asked Carl.

"You're my brother, of course I am" Tim replied.

During the drive, Matt explained how one night during their stay, they would get word on when to make their move. Carl kept asking questions that neither Tim nor Matt could answer, save for one.

"So, who thought of this whole scheme? You two?" Carl asked.

"Not us, this is all Irene." Matt said. "She started looking into all of this when she heard you may be doing this to save her from debt. She wanted to learn more about it then came across some activists who are working against Biosmart. Once you were in, she learned that almost no one does just 18 months – more like 5-10 years. Then she started planning with them and a few of us joined in."

Carl: "So you've been..."

"Yes, we've been trying to figure out how to get you out ever since you went in. Irene is up in Tahoe already getting everything ready and Marco is helping her." Tim said.

Carl exhaled deeply and said, "God she's amazing."

Somewhere around the first exit to Grass Valley they switched the subject to grilling techniques and what they wanted to grill that night. They hoped the Safeway supermarket in Tahoe City would still be open when they passed through as Tim pressed down on the gas to ensure they would make it in time.

Soon they were in Tahoe City on the north side of the lake where they stopped into Safeway to buy food for grilling that night. Tim and Matt seemed to take a longtime in the store looking at things and could not seem to decide on what to buy. This seemed out of character for both since they were the "grab it and go" kind of guys.

Back in the car, Carl asked them "What gives? When did you guys get so choosey in a damn Safeway?"

Tim looked at Matt before answering, "We were told to make this a long stop.""

"What, is Irene planning a surprise party or something?" asked Carl.

"No, they told us to stop here and take a long time so they could see if anyone followed us up from Santa Rosa" Matt said.

"Wait, so they've been following us?" Carl questioned.

Tim responded, "Yeah bro, these people are super careful."

"OK, I still want to know more about how all of this works" Carl snapped.

"We can't tell you much more because we don't know ourselves." Matt replied. "No one can know the whole plan, especially you in case you get caught. That could let Biosmart track down the whole network."

"Holy shit, these guys are serious. OK" Carl then nodded. "Can we at least stop for a beer?"

"You must be reading my mind. Sure, but we don't want to be too late meeting the kids." Tim said.

Tim then guided the black Nissan southward down route 89, winding along the western shore of Lake Tahoe toward the town of South Lake Tahoe. About 30 minutes later they turned off behind a Raley's supermarket into the South Lake Brewing company. They went inside and ordered a round of craft beers and a big plate of fries.

Carl nodded to his brother Tim and whispered, "Is this another one of those stops?"

Tim made a slightly scolding look and said, "Be cool brother, how is your beer?"

Taking the hint, Carl said "Its decent, but since when did IPAs have fruity flavors in them?" They all laughed. Matt kept checking and sending texts on his phone but said nothing.

Almost an hour later they crossed the Nevada state line and a few minutes after that pulled into a rented house in Zephr Cove on Lake Tahoe's eastern shore. Once inside, they saw Irene and Marco and exchanged hugs and unpacked the groceries and baggage. The house had an intimate backyard with a patio and a giant grill that Marco had warmed up for them. Irene put on some music, the Lithium station on satellite radio since she knows how her dad loves 90s music.

Hours later after they had eaten too much and emptied the growlers of beer they had picked up at the brewery earlier, they all ended up tucked into the plush sofas in the living room since it was getting too chilly to sit outside.

"Man, I forgot how cold it gets here at night." Marco said.

"Yeah, and I forgot what being cold is even like" Carl responded. There are certain things like smell, heat, and cold that feel like distant memories when you are in there like I am."

"Oh God, it's a good thing we are getting you out of there." Irene said with concern in her voice.

The next day they drove back to South Lake Tahoe to hang out and walk along the lake, daring each other to get into the cold water - but there were no takers.Matt kept checking his cell phone and Carl noticed that it looked like a different one that he had the day before. By now Carl stopped asking about such things since he accepted that he could not know much about it and to trust that Tim and the kids to know what they are doing.

Early that evening back at the house in Zephr Cove, Matt received a text and Irene started whispering then went to find the others.

"It's time" Irene said to her father.

Carl let out a long breath and said "OK, what do we do?"

"Leave your stuff here, put on your jacket and we'll take you someplace to get you going." she said.

Tears in his eyes, Marco ran over to hug his father. "I love you dad."

"I love you too." Carl replied. "We'll see each other again, right?"

"It may be a while Dad, and only when its safe," said Irene. "Ok, let's get moving."

Tim then turned to his brother, hugged him, and said, "See you on the other side bro."

"Thanks brother, I can't thank you enough. Please keep looking after them." Carl replied. "I don't know how I can ever repay you."

"Stop talking nonsense bro, you owe me nothing." Tim said. "Love you man."

Carl froze for a moment then hugged his brother again, "Love you too bro."

Irene, Matt, and Carl went outside and got into a silver car he had not seen before while Tim and Marco got in the black Nissan. They all pulled out together.

Matt turned the silver car north along the highway while Tim turned south toward Stateline and South Lake Tahoe.

"So where are we going? Carl asked.

"We're going shopping Dad!" Irene said impishly. "There are some great stores in Carson City!"

After about 30 minutes they were pulling into a Costco store in Carson City, Nevada. They went inside and looked around a bit, nibbling on the samples of food on the various tables inside.

After about 20 minutes of browsing the store, they went back to the car.

"More of this eh" Carl quipped.

"Da-*ad*" Irene said as she gritted her teeth and stared back at him.

Matt then drove them about three minutes away to a nearby Marshall's department store where they all went inside. Irene got a shopping cart and began to look at clothes, putting certain items into it to try on later. Matt played the bored and exasperated husband while Carl just walked along, his mind wondering about when and how he would finally make his escape and worrying about the life and family he'd be leaving behind.

*When will I see them again? How will I live? I guess this is the price of not being in there anymore.* he thought.

After about 25 minutes of shopping, Irene turned to her father and said, "I need to go to the bathroom, will you come with me and watch my cart?"

"Um, OK" Carl said.

Matt squeezed his shoulder, gave him a sincere look, then walked off to another part of the store.

Carl accompanied Irene to the bathrooms at the back of the store in a hallway off the main floor.

As soon as Irene started to open the bathroom door, a back door onto the street opened and a bearded man stood there.

"I'm Steve and I'll take you from here" the man said.

Irene turned back to her father, hugged him tightly, and started to cry. "I love you so much dad."

He kissed her cheek and held her for the longest time, but still not long enough.

"Oh, my sweet girl" He kept saying over and over "I love you."

"We need to get moving fast" Steve said, "Once they pick up you've gone offline, they'll be coming after you."

"OK, OK" Carl said "I'll see you again my beautiful. Your mother would be so proud of you. I know I am." Irene's eyes were full of tears.

Then he turned and left to go out the back door with Steve while Irene went into the bathroom to compose herself. She and Matt would stay in the area awhile longer to go shopping before heading back to Zephr Cove.

Outside, Carl saw three vans with their lights on and engines running. Steve directed him into the one in the center which seemed to have a strange cage lining the inside of it. Steve closed the door. Then, all three vans quickly drove away from the shopping center in different directions. One van headed north to Reno, the other meandered around Carson City for hours, while the third one carrying Carl went south on Route 395.

Steve motioned to Carl to hand over his phone, which he did. Steve then zipped it into a black pouch and turned back toward Carl and asked him to write down his passcode.

Carl complied then asked wryly, "So, I'm making a run for it, in a cage?"

"Correct, it's a Faraday cage." Steve replied dryly "It blocks the signals from your implants so Biosmart can't track your location."

"Ah, OK." Carl said, "You guys thought of everything."

Steve nodded and spoke. "There are food and drinks in the cooler and a blanket in case you get cold. Settle in, because it's going to be a lot of this for a few days."

The van sped into the night southward back into California before turning east on state road 359 at Mono Lake and back into Nevada. In this region there were many mobile telephone "dead zones" in which the signals from Carl's implants could not be detected if he stepped outside the van. About 45 minutes later, somewhere inside one of these zones in the Nevada desert, the van stopped, and Carl was woken up.

"Time to move again. And we'll hang onto your phone" Steve said, as Carl groaned, stretched, and stepped out of the van into the dark night.

There he saw a large camper parked next to them, the kind you see all over the western United States – it probably had paint worn by the weather and the back covered in stickers. Steve motioned toward the camper.

Silently, Carl shook his hand and stepped across into the camper.

Inside, he noticed it had a similar Faraday cage installed then turned toward the front seat where a Native American couple in their 60s greeted him. "I'm Cassandra and this is Aaron. Welcome to the rest of your life! Now settle in cuz we have a ways to go"

The camper then pulled out onto the desert highway heading east into the blackness of the night. Meanwhile, another car pulled up next to Steve's van, then he switched vehicles with the other driver.

Steve was now headed back the way they came while the van with the Faraday cage headed north toward Fallon.

## Marshall's Department Store
## Carson City, Nevada

Matt received a text on the special burner phone instructing he and Irene to start searching for Carl both inside and outside the store. He and Irene crisscrossed the store several times, asking store clerks if they had seen him and even having them make announcements looking for him.

Irene was already on the verge of tears after seeing him off with the bearded man so now she let her tears flow. She kept muttering to herself, "Oh my God, where could he be? They must have broken his brain or something." Her genuine emotions made her frantic search believable to anyone who was watching.

After about 20 minutes, she and Matt went outside to search the parking lot. By now Matt had gone from being the stoic partner reassuring her that they'd find him to letting his own genuine worry about his father-in-law's fate turn into his own shouts into the dark parking lot calling for Carl.

Appearing to be genuinely distraught, they both finally got back in their car and Irene called the police to report him missing.

"Hello 911," the operator answered.

"Hi, yes I'd like to report a missing person," Irene said.

"How long have they been missing?" The operator asked.

"Almost an hour, Irene replied.

"We can't start a search for someone after only an hour unless they are a child or have Alzheimer's or dementia. Do they have either of these?" The operator inquired.

"No, it's my Dad," Irene said. "He was in Biosmart so I think his brain may be messed up."

"I've never heard of that. I'm sending a police car to your location now." The operator replied. "Did you try to call him?"

"Of course I did!" Irene shouted. "I just want to find him." Matt touched her arm.

"OK, no need to shout. I know you're under a lot of stress," the 911 operator said.

"I'm sorry, I'm just so worried," Irene replied.

"Try to keep looking and keep an eye on your phone in case he calls. A police car should be there in about 20 minutes." The operator responded.

Irene said, "OK, thanks" and hung up the phone. She put her head in her hands against the steering wheel then whispered to Matt "good enough?"

Not smiling, Matt chuckled and said, "good enough for an Emmy, maybe even an Oscar."

The police arrived and took statements from Irene and Matt, while a small search took place. After dealing with the police, they drove back into the house in Zephyr Cove where they stayed for the night. The next day, Matt and Irene drove back to Santa Rosa.

Later the next day, Irene received a text from her father telling her that he was OK and decided to rent a car and go back to Vallejo early so he would not owe so much time to them. Irene relayed the information to the police and attempts to located him were suspended.

To anyone tracing the call, the phone was connecting from Chiloquin, Oregon where Steve sent the text. Steve then took the phone apart and threw it into Upper Klamath Lake.

**15 miles west of Ely, Nevada**

Sunlight coming into the camper started to awaken Carl. That plus the rustling and smells coming from the small kitchen.

"Good morning!" Cassandra greeted Carl when she saw him sit up on the sofa he'd been sleeping on.

"Hey," Carl replied. "Where are we?"

"We're about to pick up some friends. You hungry?" She replied.

Carl noted her evasiveness but figured he needed to play along. He responded, "Yes, I'm starving!"

Cassandra served up scrambled eggs and sausage plus some bread and coffee saying "Sorry, no room for a toaster in here."

Carl devoured his breakfast quickly and downed three cups of coffee, then asked "Is there a bathroom on this thing?"

About 30 minutes later the camper pulled into the parking lot of a diner and picked up two new passengers.

They stepped inside, took up the seats at the table across from Carl, and introduced themselves.

"Hi, I'm Sylvia and this is Tom, were here to talk to you about time at Biosmart." she said.

Carl sat back and said, "I'm not sure how much I can tell you since I was under the whole time."

Tom spoke now, "Anything you can tell us would be hugely helpful."

"I have some questions too," Carl said.

"Of course," Sylvia said. "Why don't we start there?"

"OK, first off, where are we going and what will we be doing?" Carl asked.

Sylvia looked at Tom, then said "We are taking you to a safe place in the safest way we can. Then someone will work on disabling or removing your implants. After that we'll help you restart your life."

"Will I ever see my family again?" Carl asked.

Tom answered, "Eventually, we think so. But first we need to deal with Biosmart."

"Not sure what that means, but OK," Carl said. "So, they are hunting for me now?"

"Without a doubt" Sylvia replied. "We followed you all the way from Santa Rosa to see if anyone was following you – and they were. They seemed to rely on the trackers in your implants, so they did not follow closely at all"

"Wow." Carl said.

Sylvia continued, "That is why we devised the way to extract you the way we did. We only had a 5-10 minute time window to get you out and on the road."

Carl's eyes opened wide, "Are they following us now?"

"No, we've made sure of that," Tom said.

"Ready for our questions now?" Sylvia asked.

Carl replied, "Yeah, OK."

By now they had crossed into Utah.

They spent the next two hours asking Carl about his time inside Biosmart's metaverse, the projects he worked on, and many details about his interface with P3 and other AI agents.

Once they were complete, they all relaxed and got Carl caught up on some things he had missed while he was under.

The camper stopped again at a truck stop near Salina, Utah to refill the gas tank and let Sylvia and Tom out, apparently to get into another car and leave.

By now Cassandra had taken over the wheel which allowed Aaron to take care of refueling and to buy some treats inside the truck stop. Carl asked if he could get out and stretch his legs but since they were no longer in a dead zone, he'd have to wait.

### Grand Junction, Colorado

The camper pulled into a campground in Grand Junction close to 8pm where Aaron and Cassandra hooked up to the water and electricity supply and greeted their new neighbors.

A man in a nearby camper invited Aaron to step inside of his camper and they spent about 20 minutes inside it before returning to Cassandra and Aaron's van carrying several large bags. A stern looking woman with her hair in braids also stepped into the camper.

Once inside, the man introduced himself as Kevin, the surgeon who would be working on him. The woman stood silently next to him.

"Here? Tonight?" Carl said loudly.

"Yes, here in town and no, not tonight," Kevin replied. "First, we're going to disable your implants so you can finally go outside and so we can get you into a place to do your surgery."

"Oh, thank God," Carl said.

Kevin laughed and added, "No, thank Lily!"

"I'm Lily, let's get you fixed up here."

Aaron and Cassandra left the camper and let Lily and Kevin get to work on Carl. Lily set up a series of lights in the camper that were so bright Carl though he would go blind. Kevin gave Carl a quick examination and looked at the placement of his implants. He then conferred with Lily in a language Carl did not recognize.

Kevin then said to Carl, "This shouldn't hurt but if you want something for your nerves, I can give you some medication that will relax you a good bit. We'd need to wait awhile for them to take effect though."

Carl shook his head "No, I don't want to wait any longer. Let's just do this."

Lily, the technician then took out a set of fine tools on the table and put on magnifying eyeglasses know as surgical loupe and began to remove the outer casing from one implant. To Carl, it was a bit unnerving to have someone picking at the backside of his head, so he did some of the yoga breathing his son Marco showed him a few years back.

Once the outer covering on one was removed, Lilly started picking around inside itto remove a tiny battery plus the tracking chip, the whole time seeming to mumble "hmmm, agh, ok."

After about 10-15 minutes, she had the chip and battery on a tray and started putting the cover back on.

Carl asked, "Why are you putting that back on?"

"We need to keep it clean and protected until Kevin can take them out" Lily replied.

"Ah, OK," Carl said.

Lilly then proceeded to do the same procedure on the other implant then pulled out a device to make sure no other transmitters remained within Carl's body. Once he was clear, she started putting away her tools and taking down the lights.

"So that's it?" Carl asked.

"For now, yes." Kevin said. "Why don't you go outside and have a stretch?"

"Finally!" Carl said as he headed for the camper door.

He stepped outside into the night air, raised his arms over his heads, and gave each leg a good shake.

"Oh man, I feel so stiff," Carl shouted.

"Aw stop braggin!" said an unknown older man sitting outside at a nearby camper.

Laughter was heard by a few people within earshot. And for the first time since his escape started, Carl laughed too.

### Santa Rosa, California

About a week after she last saw her father in Carson City, representatives from Biosmart called Irene on the phone and asked if they could come see her. The whole group of them had received guidance before the whole series of events that this would happen and how to be ready for it. She knew that Matt, her Uncle Tim and her would be OK but she worried about Marco. "Would he be careful enough?" she thought.

A pair of Biosmart officials came to see her at home one night to tell her that her father had not reported back in as agreed and that he needed to come back to Vallejo at once.

"But he told me he was going back there early so he would not owe more time," Irene told them.

"That is not what happened," the official said.

"He told me last week, look here it the text" Irene said as she showed them the text message from him.

"If you know where he is, you need to tell us," the other official said.

"I'm telling you, I thought he was back with you. Should I be worried? Did he get in an accident or something?" Irene asked.

"If he does not come back, his debt will pass on to you," the first official said.

Irene had been told beforehand that they would try this trick and that they were bluffing. Nonetheless, she became hysterical.

"No, no! I don't know where he is – If I did, I would tell you." Irene shrieked and started to cry. "You need to find him! Please find my father! I need to know he is safe."

Her own worry about where her father was now and what was happening to him fueled her performance and made it that much more real.

Flustered a bit by her emotional outburst, they handed her a business card with instructions to call them if she heard anything. Then they left.

Irene avoided every temptation to call or text anyone of the others with the details about this visit in case they were being monitored now. And in case they were, she texted a few friends to tell them her father had gone missing and that she was deeply worried. She also texted her brother Marco this same message, that their father was missing and to call her as soon as he heard anything.

She then started posting sad messages on social media, speaking vaguely about missing someone. The act had to be total, complete, and airtight.

That next weekend, she and Matt met Marco down near Santa Cruz at Henry Cowell Redwoods State Park. They left their cell phones in the car went on a hike dee pinto the forest and once they were far enough away from anyone else, began to share their experiences of being confronted by the Biosmart people. Uncle Tim had already told his story to Irene and Matt which they shared with Marco.

It turned out that Marco had done fine when he was visited by Biosmart and even preempted them by angrily asking where his father was since his sister had texted him that same day. He even showed them the text from Irene.

Marco's simmering anger over his father going into Biosmart and then being confronted by the people who "held him captive" as he saw it only made his emotive reactions that much more believable.

While walking under the giant redwoods they talked about how they needed to keep this just between them, otherwise their father would be in danger. Uncle Tim was the religious one and he had encouraged Matt to tell them all to pray. When Matt passed along this message, Marco rolled his eyes.

"When will we see him again?" Marco asked. No one had an answer.

Their encounters with Biosmart seemed to convince them that they did not know where their father was so the calls and visits soon stopped happening. Of course, it was true they did not know where he was, and they needed to never talk about those nights in Zephyr Cove or Carson City – not to anyone.

### Grand Junction, Colorado

Carl spent a few more days in the campground, then he was taken to a small nearby hospital where he was prepared for surgery. They did not even stop at the registration desk as Carl was quickly whisked into the surgery ward to be prepared. They placed a patient tag on his wrist and when he looked at it, it was not his name.

A nurse gave Carl a pre-op shot and the area around his implants was shaved make it clean for surgery. They also placed a cap on his head to keep the rest of his hair out of the way. Carl felt goofy but as the nurse told him, "It's better than the alternative which would be shaving your whole head." He laughed thinking about the last time he'd sported that hairstyle in basic training.

Finally, Kevin came in to check in with Carl before surgery and to explain what would be involved in the procedure.

"I'll try to get all the pieces out but if I can't do it safely, they may need to stay in," Kevin explained.

Carl winced and said, "OK doc, just do your best." Carl then thought of a question he'd been wanting to ask.

"So doc, who is paying for all of this?" Carl inquired.

"I do this surgery pro-bono and we have a benefactor that is covering the rest so relax and the anesthesiologist will be here in a few minutes." Kevin replied.

"Oh wow, thank you!" Carl said. "The last thing I needed was new medical debt."

They both shared a laugh then Kevin stepped out to prepare.

Carl's implants were taken out in a three hour surgery and the remaining holes were small enough that Kevin could stretch the skin and suture it shut. He recovered in the hospital over the next few days and was put through several tests to make sure his brain was not damaged by the removal of his implants.

Lilly collected all the pieces of the implants with the parts she had previously removed and drove away to a lab in Denver where a team was working to understand Biosmart's technology and how to disable it from a distance, perhaps through a high intensity radio frequency (HIRF) attack.

### Durango, Colorado

A few days later, Carl left the hospital and was taken to Aaron and Cassandra's house not far from Durango. There he slowly regained his strength and went through a few more cognitive tests which he passed. It was during these days Carl learned that Cassandra and Aaron were from the Navajo or as they called it, the Diné nation. They had been married for 30 years and ended up in Colorado after Aaron got a good job there.

He loved the big omelets Cassandra made every morning and every night, they made abig fire in the fireplace when Aaron and Carl shared stories from their time in the military. Carl had served as a soldier in the Army whereas Aaron served in the Marines.

"So, were you a Navajo code talker?" Carl asked.

Aaron laughed and said "No, that was only during World War II."

"Is that the language Kevin and Lilly speaking?" Carl asked.

Aaron chuckled and said, "No, wrong tribe. They are from the Pueblo."

Carl thought for a moment then asked, "Is this whole thing run by native Americans?"

"You could say that," Cassandra said as she sat down by the fire.

"Most of us are from tribes here in the southwest but there are also a few Lakota people too," Aaron said.

"Plus, we have former FBI, retired special forces, and even hippies helping us,"Cassandra added.

"Oh wow, so what brought you all together? And why are you helping me?" Carl asked. "I'm so grateful, I just wonder why me?"

Cassandra looked at Aaron before responding then asked, "What brought you to Biosmart?"

"Well, I needed the money. I inherited medical debt then took on even more when my wife was diagnosed with cancer. After she died, I decided I didn't want my kids to face that," Carl said.

"It's the same for so many of our people too. It's not like there are a lot of rich Navajos," Cassandra said. "Did you see a lot of indigenous people in there?" she asked.

"I have no idea since you never saw anyone's real face," Carl said. "I'd imagine there must be but I'm not sure."

"You look like you may have some native blood in you Carl," Aaron asked.

"I heard from my grandmother that her father was from the Cahuilla in California. We never had any papers, so the tribe never recognized us" Carl said.

"Oh, so that's why you can't take refuge with your own people," Cassandra said with a concerned look on her face.

"So the people from the tribes who became brainworkers for Biosmart, how were they afterwards?" Carl asked.

"We don't know because they never seem to come back," Aaron said.

Shocked, Carl said "Oh my God."

"Oh yes God," Cassandra nodded.

Carl replied, "My kids told me something like this but when you say it hits even harder."

"They tell the families that they've decided to stay longer to make more money," Aaron said.

"One family on the San Ildefonso Pueblo was told their daughter had died and they never got her body back," Cassandra said.

"Her family thinks she is still in there since she had an IQ of more than 150 so she was especially valuable," she added.

"How can they get away with this?" Carl asked. "Isn't this illegal?"

"It should be," Aaron said. "They've donated enough to the right politicians to give them cover. Then of course there is the fine print of the contracts people sign when they become brainworkers. It's like selling yourself to slavery."

"Besides, the law has never exactly been the friend of native people so we can't expect them to help us," Cassandra said.

"Shit," Carl said, "So this must be personal for you too."

"It sure is" Cassandra responded. "Our granddaughter Nely is in there, so we joined the cause and brought our camper with us."

His voice cracking, Aaron added, "Helping you get away brings us one step closer to bringing her home someday. Hopefully all of them someday."

"I'm so sorry," Carl said. "I'm a parent too and I can't imagine how painful that must be." Carl then went on to tell them about his children and how he missed them. He saw tears in their eyes and wanted to hug them but was not sure it would be welcomed. So, he reached for their hands.

"I can't thank you enough and I will do my best to help get her out," Carl said while holding their hands."

"That's very sweet of you Carl but it may be a bigger promise that you realize" Cassandra said, wiping tears from her eyes.

"What does it involve?" Carl asked, "Maybe I have skills they can use!"

"Nichelle will tell you that when she comes to see you," Aaron said.

Carl asked, "Who is Nichelle?"

"You'll see," Aaron said as he rocked in his chair.

Cassandra had taken Carl's sizes and bought him a few basic changes of clothes and put them into a bag for him, along with some basic toiletries.

A few days later, Nichelle arrived and took Carl away in her car. He hugged Aaron and Cassandra tightly before he left and renewed his promise to help them free Nely.

Nichelle said nothing as she waved from inside he car. Since they'd be on the road for a while, they'd have plenty of time to talk.

Carl got in and said, "So, what happens now?"

She responded, "Now we set you up with a new life,"

"How does that work?" he asked.

"First off, you'll need to stay off the grid since Biosmart will be looking for you." She spoke. "That means no smart phones and staying away from places with cameras."

"Oh yeah, facial recognition" Carl said.

"Yes" Nichelle added.

"If you get me some plastic surgery, would I be ok?" he asked.

"Sorry, but we don't have a plastic surgeon or the money for one," Nichelle said. "Besides, without radically changing your facial bone structure, it wouldn't help anyway."

"Oh wow, really?" Carl asked.

"Yes, the systems are much more sophisticated plus they have a ton of data on your face already. They probably even have a print of how you walk so they can use that to find you even if they never see your face." Nichelle replied.

"What?" Carl shouted.

"Yeah, it's called the human motion print, and it was figured out in early 2022 by some researchers in California and Germany," she said.

Nichelle continued, "The one advantage you have on that is that is that not a lot of motion print sensors are out there yet."

"Jeez, is there no privacy anymore?" Carl asked.

"Not really, unless you are out in these remote areas," Nichelle said as she pointed at the empty landscape while the car headed south into New Mexico.

"So, you're an expert on all this stuff?" Carl asked.

"Something like that," Nichelle said with a grin.

"So, you were FBI, or CIA or something like that?" Carl said.

"Carl, honey, don't ask a lady such personal questions" she replied.

"So, a new identity? What about my old one? Will I get to pick a new name?" Carl asked.

"We got all your documents from your family months ago so some day when this is all over, you can resume your original identity," she said.

This news seemed to have a soothing effect on Carl. "So, it won't be forever," Carl said.

"Not if we're successful," Nichelle stated.

She then explained the next steps.

"We're going to a friendly place in New Mexico where you'll get a new driver's license, social security card, and so on." Nichelle said.

"What will I do for work?" Carl asked.

Nichelle turned to look at him and said, "That's up to you."

"I mean, what kind of work can I do in the sticks?" he asked.

"Some grow food, some build houses, and some help the cause – but that's usually not a full-time job." Nichelle answered.

"It figures I'd end up being a farmer," Carl said.

Nichelle crinkled her nose and asked, "Why is that?"

"My Dad used to tell me I'd end up as a farmer if I did not get my grades up," Carl said.

Nichelle laughed and asked, "So what did you end up doing?"

Carl laughed and responded, "I joined the Army for the GI Bill and was in an air defense unit in Germany."

"And then?" she asked.

"Then I came home and went to San Francisco State to study industrial design." Carl said.

### Jemez Springs, New Mexico

They passed through Farmington where Nichelle took them to a drive-thru to get lunch. After they ate, she drove south and a few miles before they reached Gallup, she turned off onto a series of bumpy side roads for about two hours. If anyone was following them, they'd stand out immediately.

They finally got back on a paved road again and drove for about 40 minutes before pulling into Jemez Springs. They checked into a small hotel by the river that took cash and did not ask questions. Someone arrived that night to take Carl's photo for his new ID cards. Then he and Nichelle lazed about the next day until the person who took his photos returned with a manila envelope he gave to Nichelle, who handed him a fat envelope in return.

Nichelle then took Carl in her SUV up into the Jemez National Forest and parked at a picnic area. Since it was a weekday in late October, they were all alone. They sat down and Nichelle opened the envelope.

"OK, so your new name will be Joesph Yellowtail" she said and put his new driver's license on the table."

"An Indian name?" Carl asked.

"Well, you pass for native, and your kids said you have some native blood so this will help you blend in here more," Nichelle said.

"Yeah, so Carl Vigil becomes Joseph Yellowtail," Carl said. "I think I'll go by Joe."

"Sounds good Joe," she said. "And here is your birth certificate, high school diploma,and associate degree from Central New Mexico Community College. There are a few more things in here too."

"But I have a bachelor's degree in industrial design!" He protested.

"And that is what Biosmart will be looking for so you can't just pop up doing the same work with the same qualifications. It's no way to hide you," Nichelle said.

Carl still looked displeased.

Nichelle looked him in the eye and said, "When you're running for your life, the first thing you have to give up is the life you had." Carl's demeanor softened. She explained a few more about his new life until finally he said, "I think I need a nap."

The next day, Nichelle drove him over to the San Ildefonso Pueblo to meet some people, She reminded him to use his new name. They parked near a big house and entered to find several people waiting to greet them. Carl also smelled food.

"Welcome,"said a man who seemed to be in charge. He introduced himself as Daniel and next to him was his wife, Rose. Daniel was a tribal elder and host of this lunch meeting. He and Rose were also the parents of Raven, the Biosmart worker who supposedly died.

"I'm so sorry," Carl said. "My name is Joe and it's an honor to meet you."

Another couple introduced themselves as coming from the Tesuque Pueblo. Their son had been in Biosmart for years already. The last two were from the Pojoaque Pueblo and their daughter had been in for three years and was already two years overdue to come home.

Nichelle had told him on the way about the importance of meeting these parents and how he represented hope to them. "So be that hope" she told him. Carl was already missing his own family and had no idea when he would see them again. He could relate to a lot of their pain. They spent a long afternoon eating and asking him what life was like as a brainworker in Biosmart's metaverse. He also answered questions about what it was like to be directly connected to an AI.

"It's a powerful feeling but it never stops feeling weird," he told them. Carl started to tell them about his own family, but Nichelle stopped him.

"Joe, we can't go there." She admonished.

"Why not?' Rose said. "We keep secrets better than any white people do."

Nichelle could not help but laugh. "OK," she said, "but no names or places."

Carl then continued talking about his family; his parents, and their long illnesses, losing his wife to cancer well before her time and how proud he was of his son and daughter. They all nodded, and their faces softened even more.

"We all need this to end so our families will be together again," said the Tesuque mother.

"Amen to that," Carl said.

That night they wanted to do a short ceremony for Carl to give him protection in the days ahead. It was not something that was ordinarily done unless someone was marrying into the community. The Pueblo people were especially secretive given since their bad experiences with white people since the late 1500s and they were also secretive around even other Pueblo tribes. So, they made a circle around him and chanted their prayers of protection in their own Tewa languages while Nichelle watched from across the room.

Carl left that night, touched not only by the stories of their children in Biosmart, but also their warm hospitality. He felt a connection to them, and a growing sense of commitment to helping the cause that had freed him. As Carl waved goodbye from the SUV as Nichelle drove him away, he could not help but wonder if this was their intention behind this visit.

They drove a short way and ended up at a small roadside hotel in White Rock where Nichelle bade him farewell. She gave him some cash and a prepaid 'dumb phone.'

"In the coming days you'll be given a choice, to quietly make a new life up here and wait for us to take down Biosmart, or to join us and help to make that day come faster." She spoke.

"Doesn't sound like much of a choice to me, I'm in." Carl said.

"Someone will be here to get you tomorrow. Her name is Kendra." Nichelle said. "Good luck and if I see you again, it means we're making progress." Then Nichelle drove away.

### White Rock, New Mexico

Carl heard a knock at the door of his motel room the next morning. Since he was now suspicious of everything, he hesitated to answer the door. Besides, he had to pull on a pair of gray sweatpants too.

"It's me, Kendra," said a voice through the door. Carl opened the door and said, "Sorry, trying to be careful."

Kendra, dressed in a denim jacket, motioned that she wanted to step into the room. Carl stepped aside and let her enter, her long strawberry blonde hair wafting past him as she walked in.

Carl introduced himself as Joe and she responded, "I'm Kendra, your local guide." Carl had a curious look on his face now.

Kendra went on, "Today we're going on a tour of the area, then I'll take you to where you'll be settled for a while."

"Sounds good," Carl said. "Can we eat first?"

"Of course!" Kendra said.

Carl packed the small bag Cassandra had given him and followed her to an old FordF150 truck. Once inside, Kendra guided the truck out of the motel parking lot onto the road which ran along under stony cliffs. They stopped at a nearby food truck called the Hungry Bear where they ordered breakfast burritos and coffee then sat at a picnic table nearby.

Carl felt the warm sun on his face as he looked over at Kendra with a glint in his eye. He had either been mourning Giselle, living inside of Biosmart, or on the run the last three years and it was the first time he felt alive again. "So,what is your story?" Carl asked.

Kendra let out a giggle and said, "Not wasting any time are you!"

"I didn't mean it like that," he said. "I mean, what got you involved in all of this?"

"All of what?" she asked.

Carl then realized that Kendra may not know his whole story and for their safety he'd need to keep it that way.

"Living off the grid, all this stuff." He said.

"Isn't that why you're here?" she said.

"Yeah, it is." He said sheepishly.

Kendra thought for a moment then spoke, "Everyone comes to this for their own different reasons. Some really value their privacy, some are on the run from a bad relationship or the law, and some are just fiercely independent. Which one are you?"

"I just want a new start without all the BS," Carl answered.

"And how deep do you want to go?" she asked.

"I'm not sure yet, I still don't know how deep or shallow it's possible to go. I guess I have a lot to learn before I know the answer to that," Carl said.

"That's the right attitude I think," Kendra said. "There are a growing number of people trying to escape the world of surveillance, so you'll be in good company."

Once they had finished their breakfast, they refilled their coffees and got back in the truck and drove off. As they passed through Espanola, Kendra remarked that it was the heroin addiction capital of America.

"No kidding?" Carl asked.

"Yep" she said, "This is how so many people try to escape – with drugs."

"Damn," Carl said.

Kendra continued, "It's a sign of a sick society that so many people are trying to escape it. I used to think I could change it, but it was like throwing a pebble against a wave."

"Maybe we can't stop the whole wave, but we can at least help some people from getting hit by it," Carl said.

"Hmmm, I like that." Kendra sighed.

They drove onward and chatted about life and society, finding much common ground. Eventually they passed through Taos and headed north into El Prado where they turned in at a sign which said "Earthship Visitor Center." Before heading inside the visitor center, Kendra turned to Carl and said, "This is one of a few options which you may or may not like."

Once inside, Carl learned all about Earthships, homes made from mostly recycled materials that enabled people to live off-grid. They often had their own in-home nurseries for growing food, used solar power, had their own wells, and used natural sewage treatment.

The Earthship community even had its own academy to train people how to design and build them. Carl thought this could be a possible area of work for him. Everyone was very kind and welcoming, but it somehow did not feel like a place he would fit in.

They later took a tour of an Earthship home and Carl noticed they had a television and internet service. "Off grid eh," he chuckled as he and Kendra walked back to the truck.

"Like I said, everyone chooses for themselves how deep they want to go," Kendra said.

"I mean, everyone is nice and it looks cool but what do they do for work?" he asked.

"A lot of them come here with their own money already," Kendra responded.

"So, it's off-grid living for the privileged" Carl opined.

"Yeah, it's a fair point," Kendra said. "They are also visited by the media all the time, so this is not ideal if you want to real privacy."

"Hmmm,"Carl grunted. "It's a cool idea but these may not be my people."

"Yeah, they're too little bougie for me too" she chuckled and smiled.

"You ready to see more?" Kenda asked.

"OK, but can we eat first?" Carl said.

"Gawd, you're always hungry!" she laughed.

They drove back into Taos and ate lunch enchiladas at roadside place called Orlando's. Carl saw signs pointing toward Taos Pueblo and asked if they could go see it.

"It's a beautiful and moving place and you need to be in the right frame of mind to see it. Plus, today we have more places to see. Another time?" she said. Carl nodded.

As they got back in the truck, Kendra said, "I heard you are a vet so there is a place you may like."

"Yeah, I was. But not all vets mix well together," Carl replied.

"I think these vets may be more your tribe," Kendra said.

Carl started to think that if he was asked to prove he was a vet, he had no papers to prove it since he was living as Joe Yellowtail now. He would need to look through the envelope he got from Nichelle later to see if they had included anything like that.

After about 20 minutes they pulled into the hamlet of Carson, New Mexico where a grouping of home sites were in various stages of completion.

When they got out of the truck, Kendra walked off to find the person who was supposed to show them around. Carl stood outside the truck and took in the views. There were large greenhouses growing plants of all kinds and a large flagpole with an American flag flapping in the breeze. Looming across the vast expanse of grasslands were mountains on all sides.

A few minutes later Kendra returned and introduced him to a man who said, "Welcome to Off Grid Vets, I'm Ray."

"Off Grid Vets?" Carl asked.

"Yeah, OGV. We're a bunch of vets making our own way and healing from the trauma we went through. Are you a vet?" Ryan asked.

"Yes, I am, and I was in Desert Storm but not any of the other wars," Carl said.

"Welcome home brother," Ray said and shook his hand, then pulled him closer for a hug.

"Can you tell Joe how things work here?" Kendra asked. Carl had been uneasy about introducing himself since he was not used to lying and was glad Kendra did this for him.

"Sure, let's take a walk so I can show you," Ray said.

"Here you can literally rebuild your life, starting with your own home and growing your own food. Best of all, you do it in a community of other vets who are doing the same thing and helping each other," Ray said as they walked toward a small home being built by hand.

Ray explained how he bought 60 acres in this area in order to help other veterans build their own homes and live off the grid, healing and helping each other with the support of a group of volunteers from Taos and the surrounding area.

Staring at the barren dirt where these homes were being built, Carl thought about the home he had to sell in Santa Rosa to pay down his debt. And even that was not enough.  He and Giselle raised their kids in that home and the gut punch of pain of how much he'd lost hit him again.

He took a steadying breath and turned his back to the vista.

"Hey, are you OK Joe?" Ray asked.

"Yeah, just so much hitting me now." Carl said.

"You're not alone man. Everyone needs some time to process how they got here," Ray said as he touched Carl's shoulder.

"This place is not the end, it's a new beginning," Kendra added.

"But it can be your forever home if you want that too," Ray reassured him.

They stayed awhile longer as Ray and a few others at off Grid Veterans explained to Carl how he could join them and earn a living at the same time.  The sun was getting low in the sky and the cool autumn breeze started to quicken.

As they walked back to the truck, Carl told Ray he would think about it and let him know.

"Thanks for showing me everything Ray. Even if I don't end up here, I'll want to help regardless," Carl said as he stepped into Kendra's Ford.  Ray waved goodbye to them then put on some work gloves and went back to help dig out the foundation for a new home site.

As Kendra drove Carl back toward Taos, he asked, "So which one of these places do you live in?"

Kendra smiled and said, "That is our last stop today."

They drove back south toward Espanola and Carl said, "Please tell me that's not where we are going."

Kendra giggled and said, "Nope, someplace much better."

Just before Espanola, they turned right over the Rio Grande then across one of its tributaries, the Chama River as they headed northwest down a beautiful valley full of green farmland.

They passed by the village of Medanales then through the town of Abiquiu. About a mile later, Kendra guided the truck onto a dirt road and past a series of vegetable gardens then into a hamlet of makeshift cabins under a canopy of shade trees.

"Here we are, home of the Damish!" Kendra said with a hint of delight.

"Damish?" Carl asked.

"Yeah, the Digital Amish – Damish!" she replied.

"Um, OK" Carl said with an impish grin. "So why are the lights on?"

"We're only digitally Amish silly, we still need electricity!" She laughed.

"You need to explain all of this to me," Carl said as he stepped out of the truck with the bag slung over his shoulder.

"Don't worry, we will." Kendra replied.

"We?" Carl asked.

"You'll see, come on inside." Kendra urged him.

They walked into one of the larger cabins at the front of the hamlet and several people were sitting playing cards.

"What have you brought us here Kendra?" A 60-something man with a long beard called from a table.

"Not what, but who!" Kendra replied. "Everyone, this is Joe. He's staying with us, at least for a while."

"Hey Joe! Welcome to Zipperhead, I'm Fred!"said the older gentleman.

"Thanks, and what's Zipperhead?" Carl asked.

"You know, from the song Punk Rock Girl. I'm Angie," said a woman with a buzz haircut and arms covered in tattoos.

"Because here its always the 1990s!" said another man who was at the table playing cards. "I'm Jeff."

"Thanks everybody," Carl said as he surveyed the room. It looked like this was a community space since it was stacked with board games, books, vinyl records, CDs, musical instruments, tables, and what seemed to be a kitchen in one corner. There was also a fireplace and a small stack of wood along one wall.

"Since you're new here you can help us chop some firewood tomorrow, so we'll be ready for the winter," said a middle-aged woman with sparkly eyes. "I'm Laura and welcome to the rest of your life."

"People keep saying that to me, does it mean something?" Carl asked.

"So, he doesn't know?" Laura said looking at Kendra.

"He knows, but not the whole story." Kendra answered.

"Well Joe, this something we say to people who are new to what we call the Underground Railroad for Digital Freedom."

"Hmm, cool." Carl replied. "So how does it work? Where does everyone come from""

"First rule is you don't ask people about their past and they don't tell you about it unless they want to, which is not a problem for Fred," Kendra replied. They all laughed and Fred mimed feeling like he had been stabbed in the chest.

"Yeah, he'll talk your ear off." Angie chimed in.

"The way it works is that we all want to live away from the world of constant surveillance. You know, cell phones, facial recognition, credit cards, and soon. Hell, even your car spies on you now." Laura said.

She went on, "so we live with no smartphones, no WIFI, no newer cars, and we live on cash."

"See, just like the 90s!" Jeff chimed in. "You don't have a smart phone on you, do you?" He asked.

"Oh hell no," Carl replied.

"OK everyone, I need to show Joe to his sleeping place now. Then we can come back," Kendra said.

"Makin' the moves on him already?" Fred joshed.

"Don't worry Fred, you'll always be my number one." Kendra laughed as she led Carl out of the community cabin and onto a path where he could hear the river.

"It's so quiet and peaceful here." Carl said as they walked.

"Quiet yes, but not always peaceful." Kendra said.

"Why is that?" Carl asked.

"Put a bunch of independent minded people in one place and there's bound to be friction at some point," Kendra replied.

They came to a row of cabins and Kendra took him inside the second one, turning on the light. Carl saw it was essentially one room with a small bathroom and shower in one corner, separated from the rest of the space only by a shower curtain. There was a bed in one corner with the sheets on it undone and a bunch of old clothes hanging on hooks. There was a fireplace in one corner but only a few logs in the firewood stack. There were also shoes and work boots near the door. The whole place felt slightly chilly.

"This place used to be Maurice's, but he left us a few months ago," Kendra said. "It can be yours if you pull your weight and you're not a psycho."

Carl laughed and said, "Not a psycho. "What if Maurice ends up coming back?" He asked.

"Well, he passed away so I wouldn't worry about that." She said. Carl paused for a minute to consider that he was moving into a dead man's house, and that he may have even died on the bed they wanted him to sleep on.

"Oh, don't worry, Maurice wanted his place and his stuff to go to whoever showed up here next." Kendra said. "He was generous like that."

"He sounds like a great guy," Carl said.

"He really was," Kendra replied. "He was one of the founders of this place and had a hand in building all these homes."

"Did anyone change these sheets after he died?" Carl asked.

"I'm not sure, but just so you know he did not die in this bed." Kendra responded.

"OK, maybe I can settle in and sleep. Is that cool?" Carl asked.

"Sure, and if you need anything my cabin is the one next door on the right as you leave this door," Kendra said as she gave him a hug and left.

Carl turned off the top light then flicked on a lamp near the bed and sat down and took off his shoes and socks. He sat on the bed for a long while thinking about everything that happened over the past week or so. He did not seem to know what day it was or even what time it was. All he knew was that he felt cold, so he rolled up under the sheets and comforter and soon fell asleep.

### Zipperhead, New Mexico

Carl woke up the next day feeling stiff and cold. "So, this is the rest of my life," he thought to himself.

He put on a fresh change of clothes, not wanting to try the shower in the chilly air. Then he walked out into the sunlight and smelled the fresh air. "Maybe it's not so bad," he thought.

Carl wandered a bit and saw chicken coops near one edge of the large vegetable garden and a good-sized greenhouse. He then found his way into the community cabin where Angie was boiling water and

Laura was eating oatmeal alongside four new faces he had not met yet. Everyone introduced themselves and made "Joe" feel welcome.

"You hungry?" Laura asked.

"Oh yeah," Carl replied.

"Then go help yourself," Laura said as she motioned toward the kitchen.

Carl walked over to the kitchen where Angie poured boiling water into a teapot. There he saw a bowl of uncooked eggs, peppers, mushrooms, onions, and a coffeepot next to an empty skillet on the stove. As he started to make himself a small omelet, he was conscious not to use too many eggs since they were sharing with him, and he did not want to make a bad impression.

The smells and sounds of cooking breakfast made him nostalgic for the days when he would cook breakfast for his kids on weekends. It was the only time Giselle let him run the kitchen, she said because it was the only meal he knew how to cook. These bittersweet thoughts made him sigh as he turned the omelet over.

He poured himself some coffee from the pot and took a plate with his breakfast over to a table where Laura was sitting with Angie. The group he met a few minutes ago, a couple with dreadlocks and a few middle-aged men in t-shirts sat at a nearby table.

"Good morning," Carl said. "Where is Kendra?"

"Oh hey," Angie said. "She is at work in town."

"Nice. Think I can find some work nearby?" Carl asked.

"Oh, don't worry, you will. A big strong man like you," Laura added.

Carl laughed and tucked into his breakfast with gusto while Angie and Laura explained more about how life at Zipperhead works. He would be expected to do his share, which meant gardening, chopping firewood, helping to build and fix up homes, and helping to pay the water and light bills. There were two trucks that everyone could use so if he found a job he'd need to either be dropped off by someone or drop someone else off on his way in and out. Somehow, they all seemed to make it work.

Laura told him how Zipperhead was just one of many small Damish communities popping up all over the western US. There were four communities in New Mexico, six in Colorado, and a few more in Wyoming and Utah.

"People are sick of having their whole lives being monitored and manipulated. At least here we can be more free," Laura said.

"Amen sister," Angie chimed in.

"And if you really need to use the internet for something, we go to the library in Abiquiu."Laura said.

Once they finished breakfast and most of the people had shuffled out for the day, Jeff stopped in to pour a cup of coffee and said, "Hey new guy, you've got the dishes today."

"And then you can help me chop firewood," Fred said from a corner. Carl wondered how Fred had snuck in without him seeing.

Carl then set about washing the dishes and pans and instead of it feeling like a chore, it made him feel normal again. Something about the ritual of scrubbing, rinsing, and putting dishes and pans on the drying rack felt more like a meditation. He had not done any of these things in so long that he felt refreshed by it. Lost in his own thoughts,he also barely noticed that Fred had been chattering away at him from the corner.

Once he was done, Fred took him out to a group of felled trees that had been dragged to the edge of the vegetable garden. Fred picked up a chain saw and handed an axe to Carl with a grin as if to say, "New guy gets the dirty work."

Fred then proceeded to saw the trees into smaller cylinders and half-cylinders that Carl could chop into firewood. Since Carl finished his task much sooner, he then sat down and started to regale Carl with story after story of his life and the short history of Zipperhead.

Carl's hands felt sore, and he started to take longer breaks between chopping logs. He had lost a lot of strength and stamina in Biosmart, and it would take a while to get it back.

"Getting tired already Joe?" Fred asked.

"Nah, just feeling stiff and my hands are blistering." Carl answered.

"Why don't you grab some work gloves?" Fred asked him.

"I didn't know you had them," Carl said.

"Well, you never asked, they're in that box over there!" Fred replied and pointed to a box on the side of a nearby cabin.

*Man, this guy is a piece of work* Carl thought as he went to grab the gloves.

Carl continued to chop wood all the way into the early afternoon as Fred would not stop talking. He told him about how to avoid facial recognition cameras and other means of surveillance outside their little hamlet. If Carl had met Fred a few years earlier, he'd think he was a looney conspiracy theorist but in his current situation, Carl was grateful for his wisdom.

Once he went to find lunch, Carl went back to his room to lay down. But before that he looked at the clothes left by Maurice and found that some of them fit, including a nice warm coat for the winter. Sadly, none of the boots or shoes did.

Carl also took another look inside the envelope Nichelle gave him and found a bankcard for the Nusenda Credit Union with a post it note on the back with a four digit number. *That must be the PIN,* he thought.

He put it into the small wallet Aaron and Cassandra had given him alongside his new driver's license and library card.

Instead of eating lunch he asked Laura how to find a Nusenda branch and if he could take the truck to go there. She was heading into Espanola and offered to give him a ride. She also told him that if he walked into a bank branch, he would be on a surveillance camera. "Is that what you want?" She asked.

"No, but wouldn't an ATM be the same?" Carl replied.

"Not if you wear a hat and sunglasses," she said. "Here, wear these," she said as she handed him some large, rounded women's sunglasses.

"I can't wear these," Carl spat out.

"You can if you want to get money out," Laura said. "The rounder shape covers your cheekbones more which makes you harder to pick out." They got into the truck where Laura donned a cowboy hat and offered Carl a wide-brimmed hat to go with the sunglasses.

"You want me to look like Georgia O'Keeffe?" Carl asked jokingly.

"Maybe. You know she used to live in this area, right?" Laura asked as the truck turned onto the road.

"Yeah, I know," Carl said. "Fred must have told me three times already."

Laura chucked and said, "Yeah, he's a talker."

"Why do some people do that?" Carl asked. "He never seems interested in anyone else's life but talks nonstop about his own."

"Well look, he's old" Laura said. "And some people can't stop thinking about their glory days since that is all he's got."

"Yeah, but he's still alive, right? Isn't he making any new memories?" Carl asked.

"He is, but everything is better when you're young so maybe he wants to remember that,"Laura said.

"It's just kinda sad," Carl sighed.

"Yeah,so make sure you don't end up like that. I always try to be present and live in the now," Laura offered.

Carl nodded and said, "That is some great advice."

Later, they pulled into an ATM in Espanola where Carl jumped out with his new hat and big sunglasses on. Laura also gave him a long coat to wear so his body shape would look more ambiguous on any cameras. Feeling slightly ridiculous, Carl put the card into the ATM, entered the PIN from the post-it note, and did a balance inquiry. He was surprised to see that he had $12,000 in the account and wondered who put up the money it in there for him. Irene and Marco? The group that was helping him, or was it the mysterious benefactor?

Marco tried to withdraw $500 but was rejected since the daily limit was $400. So he withdrew $400 in cash and walked back to the truck. As he closed the door he turned to Laura and said, "Lunch is on me!"

Over the next several weeks, Carl slowly started to integrate into the Zipperhead community and found some day jobs in the local area where he worked alongside a few others from their group. They got paid in cash at the end of each day and played card games each night or read books. He did not miss television at all, but he was aching to contact his kids to let them know he was OK. He wanted to ask Kendra about it, but he was not sure how much she knew about his past.

One November night he sat next to Kendra near the fireplace after everyone else had gone to bed and was having a hard time hiding his attraction to her. They chatted late into the night, and he found out that Kendra had kids too but lost custody of them after her second rehab when she also lost her nursing license. She had not seen them in 15 years, and she wondered if they even remembered her. Her sense of shame and loss was palpable, and her eyes teared up.

Carl felt bad and put his arm around her in an embrace that she did not reject. He thought briefly about kissing her but did not want ruin the vibe. He told her how he missed his own kids and how he wishes he could talk to them, so they knew he was ok.

"It's OK, they know you are safe and fine," she said.

Carl released the hug and sat upright, saying "How do you know that?"

"I know that Joe is not your real name and that you are very special to the cause," Kendra said.

"Whoa, really?" Carl asked.

She nodded as if to say, "yes."

"My name is Carl," he said.

"I didn't know that but please don't tell anyone else here, especially Fred the blabbermouth." She replied.

They then hugged again, and she told him that at some point the cause would ask him to go back to Biosmart to help shut them down.

Carl hugged her close and said, "I know that day will come, and I'll be ready."

"OK, good," she said. "Now go to sleep."

They both left and walked back to their cabins, sharing one last long hug. But they did not kiss. Not yet

Carl and Kendra found their way back to the OGV village and helped them to dig a new well. Ray and the other vets were most grateful and asked Carl if he wanted to take over one of the home sites one day.

"You'd need to raise $5,000 to build here but there are people who can help, even the VA." Ray said. Carl knew that he could not apply for any kind of VA benefits as Joe Yellowtail, but he did have enough money in the Nusenda account, so he told Ray he'd think about it.

Carl enjoyed a subdued Thanksgiving and Christmas at Zipperhead, and he finally kissed Kendra on New Year's Eve. The wait had been so long that she was becoming impatient. Carl had wanted to take it slow since he felt guilty kissing another woman even though Giselle had been dead for three years. But he felt a peaceful closeness with Kendra that he could not resist. He also remembered what Giselle told him not a week before she died, to "Please find love again. I want you to love again."

He teared up anytime he thought of that moment. He had a river of love waiting to burst from his heart, so he finally let his guard down and let himself show Kendra how he felt. When they finally kissed, he felt like an idiot for not doing it sooner. They made love and cuddled all weekend in her cabin and when they walked into the community cabin for breakfast together looking happy, Laura and Angie smiled and said "Finally!"

In early January, a big white Suburban pulled up to the worksite where Carl was painting the inside of a building and two familiar faces stepped out, Nichelle and Steve. Nichelle's hair was in long cornrows and Steve's beard was collecting the snow from the flurries in the air.

They brought Carl a coffee and asked him to join them in the SUV. Once inside, they asked him, "So, are you ready to help the cause?"

Carl replied, "Yes, I am. Where and when do I start?"

Nichelle spoke first, "Your experience in industrial design and knowledge of some parts of their Vallejo facility could be very valuable to us. What else do you think you can do?"

Carl had been thinking long and hard about everything he remembered about what he was allowed to see inside Biosmart.

"I also did design on building safety systems, so I remember what models and brands of equipment I saw there. Maybe that could help, "Carl said.

"Maybe it could," Steve answered. "What about the workings of the AI itself?"

"I told all of that to Tom and Sylvia already," Carl said.

"Yes, but you may know even more," Steve replied.

"We're also curious how your brain may have changed while you were in there, like maybe you became extra smart too." Nichelle said.

"I don't know about that, but I am able to solve puzzles like ten times faster than I used to. Everyone is mad at me here because I've run through all the crossword books and I kick their asses at Trivial Pursuit," Carl said.

"Hmm, maybe there is something there." Nichelle opined.

"Either way, we need you to come with us to Colorado, now." Steve said.

"OK, but I need to say goodbye to someone." Carl said

"Don't worry, she knows already." Nichelle said.

"But I want to see her again. I can't lose everyone in my life," Carl pleaded. "Besides, I need to get the rest of my papers from my cabin."

"We have them already," Nichelle said as she held up his backpack and handed it to him.

"Don't worry, you'll see her again soon," Steve said as she pulled the vehicle onto the road and headed north toward the Colorado border.

They ate at a roadside café en route and about an hour after sunset they arrived in a suburb of Boulder. They took him to the home of a hippie preacher named Roger where he was set up in the guest room. He wished he could see Kendra again and hoped it would not be too long before he could. He also wondered what 'the cause' was going to ask him to do.

He slept fitfully that night and woke up to the smell of breakfast wafting through Roger's house.

Hearing Carl stirring, Roger called out "You hungry?"

"Always!" Carl replied.

They ate a big breakfast and Roger talked with Carl about spirituality, digital freedom, and human free will.

"It's almost like that movie The Matrix was a prophecy," Roger said.

"How so?" Carl asked.

"More like the Truman Show actually," Roger replied. We're living in a world where our every move and decision is monitored by the same people who want to sell things to us, be they products or political views."

Roger went on, "How do we even know if the choices presented to us are the only ones available? Are we really making our own choices if we're being manipulated every step of the way?"

"Oh man," Carl said. "I know that feeling in ways you can't even imagine."

"It's like the Hindu concept of Maya, except its manufactured by humans with the power and resources to d." Roger said, then took another sip of coffee.

"Man, you are not like any priest or preacher I've ever met!" Carl said.

"Yeah,I get that a lot," Roger said with a grin. "You want some more toast?"

After breakfast, Roger drove Carl to a warehouse in Boulder next to a climbing gym called The Spot. Once inside, Carl saw Steve, Nichelle, Kevin, and three others sitting around a table.

Come on in Joe, let's get started. "So, even here they want to use my fake name,"Carl thought to himself.

"Our plan is to break into the facility and get Raven out of there. Since Biosmart claimed she is dead, proving she is alive gives her family the legal grounds to sue them and expose the company for what they are," Nichelle said.

"Why can't we get them all out?" Carl asked.

"Its too risky," Kevin said. "Even getting Raven out we'll be at our limits to keep her alive and not damage her brain."

"Yeah, but you used to work there, don't you know how it all works?" Carl asked.

"I did, but like you I only got to see part of the place, they keep everything very compartmented." Kevin said.

The group had an overhead photo of the Biosmart facility in Vallejo on the table and were trying to map out where each component of the facility's interior was located. It was tricky to figure out and the group was stumped.

Carl asked if they had figure out yet where all the utility inputs and outputs were located since that would help him to decipher what was inside. Once they pointed those out, Carl was able to help them draw in the possible locations for key systems in the building based on his industrial design experience. He then showed them where he thought the medical intake area was, which Kevin confirmed. He also pointed out a few hallways and doors that could be offices or storage closets.

Through this process of accounting for possible known spaces, they were able to narrow down where the computer mainframes where they thought the brainworkers were 'stored.' They went back and forth on possible locations of each over the course of a week and had major arguments over each possible layout.

Finally, they figured they'd need to fly a thermal imaging drone over the facility to solve the argument. The colder area was most likely the computer mainframe and the warmer one would be the room where the brainworkers were held. They figured the facility could hold around 120-170 brainworkers at any given time.

Two of the team left that day, presumably to find the right drone to fly over the building. The rest stayed to brainstorm and solidify a plan. Kevin mentioned that if there was a safety hazard, the protocol was to disconnect the brainworkers and wheel them into a side parking lot, presumably still asleep.

"We still don't know what that would do to any of them, but we'll have to take the risk," Kevin said.

Steve had learned by eliciting from some of Biosmart's cyber team that the mainframe could also be rapidly backed up onto a special hard drive located in a small secure building within the compound but far enough away to be safe from any hazards in the building. It was backed up every six hours so they would want to grab this while they rescued Raven.

"So, how do we make them activate that protocol?" Nichelle asked.

"What if there is a fire?" Carl asked.

"We can't risk burning the brainworkers to death," Kevin said.

"But we won't need to," Carl said.

"What do you mean?" Steve asked.

"I mean, we make them think there is a fire, then they'd follow that protocol, right?" Carl asked.

"Theoretically, but how do we do that?" Nichelle said.

"We set off their fire sensors, but not with fire." Carl said. They all gave him puzzled stares.

"Look, every industrial building like this has fire sensors and fire extinguishing systems and they are all connected to the internet." Carl said.

He went on, "I saw it in my work that you can find any piece of industrial technology on the internet, I mean each individual sensor – in the world. As long as it's on the internet."

"No way," Steve said.

"Yes way," Carl responded. "Here, give me your laptop and I'll show you."

Steve slid his laptop over to Carl who typed for a minute then turned the computer around for all to see. On the screen they saw a website called Shodan, 'the world's first search engine for internet-connected devices.'

"So, if we can find it and hack it, we can make them think a fire is happening?"Steve asked.

"Yep," Carl said.

"Genius," Nichelle said.

"OK, but how do we know which ones are theirs?" Steve asked.

"I recognized the fire sensors they had as the Univario FMX 5000 IR model when I was in the medical area. There is no reason why they would use something different in the mainframe or brainworker room." Carl said.

"How do you know this stuff?" Steve asked.

"Dude, I work in industrial design and engineering. Well, at least I used to. This stuff is kinda routine." Carl said.

Nichelle said "OK, so if we can hack in and set off the fire sensors, they'll launch their protocol and start moving brainworkers out of the building. But what if there is no smoke? They'll just move them all right back in. We also will need to get into that gate with a vehicle to carry Raven out. She won't be able to walk, will she?"

"Nope," Kevin said.

"Maybe, or maybe not." Steve opined. "If the fire department shows up, they'll have to let them in and that opens the gates for us. We'll need to take advantage of the confusion and maybe use some smoke canisters to make it believable and cover our exit."

"OK, this is a good concept so far." Nichelle said. "Let's work on it more next week."

That weekend, Carl went on a hike in the mountains with Roger and they talked more about life and the cause they were supporting. Roger had no idea what Carl was part of planning, and it was best to keep it that way. He offered to take Carl to a yoga class in town, but Carl declined, not wanting to be exposed to any cameras.

The following Monday, the team met again in the warehouse. Steve had conferred with some hackers he found on the dark web who helped him find the sensor suite at Biosmart. It turned out the device passwords were still using the manufacturer's default password of 123456.

"We got lucky; the installers must have been lazy" Steve said as he presented these findings to the group. Steve also presented a plan to have a small team plan to enter the grounds in an ambulance right behind the local fire services that showed up. This way they could enter unhindered and have a decent cover to extract Raven from the facility.

Steve also outlined how every vehicle they used will need to be checked for GPS tracking devices and have them removed in addition to changing the license plates to make their movements less traceable after the fact. He would obtain large magnets with a different ambulance company logo to cover any existing markings on the ambulance they rented.

He also mentioned how they'd need to wear surgical masks and clear glasses to make them less likely to be seen on any facial recognition cameras. "Man, this guy thinks of everything." Carl thought to himself.

"This is good progress," Nichelle said. "But we also need that backup drive so someone needs to grab it. And if we can't grab it, we need to render their system inoperable so they can't plug the people back in."

"I thought we just wanted to rescue Raven and expose them?" Carl asked.

"The benefactor wants it so they can shut them down once and for all," Nichelle answered.

"I don't think we have the resources to pull that off right now," Steve said.

"I'll get you the resources Steve." Nichelle responded.

Steve also reported that the two team members who left previously had obtained a thermal drone and were heading to Vallejo to check the place out.

"Why do we need to know that if they'll be bringing them all out anyway?" Carl asked.

"Because they don't all come out at once and we may need to go in there and find Raven," Kevin said.

"How will we even identify her?" Nichelle asked.

"We have photos from her family plus she has a tattoo of a Tewa symbol on her right shoulder. Her parents hated it when she got it but now it's very helpful to us," Kevin said.

"OK, good. Let's get to planning. How soon can we pull this off Steve?" Nichelle asked.

"I'd say we need 4-5 weeks and about thirty thousand in cash to procure what we need and be ready to pay off a few people here and there." Steve responded.

"Am I going on this?" Carl asked.

"If you want to, but it's very risky and you're not trained for this." Steve said.

"I want in, I can drive the ambulance." Carl said.

"OK, but we'll need to rehearse a lot of stuff before we can pull this off." Steve replied.

"Steve you take your team to get the extraction plan ready and I'll start working on some media contacts so we can show Raven to the world once you free her," Nichelle said.

"If she is still alive," Kevin added.

"Roger boss," Steve said.

Steve took Carl back to Roger's place to pick up his things then they met three others to pile into a van headed for California. Carl was excited to be a part of this plan but also started having nightmares of being plugged back in if he were caught. He was also missing Kendra and wished he could call her.


## Sacramento, California

After stopping at a shabby roadside motel in Nevada the day before, the team drove onward and eventually went through Sacramento and over to a nearby area that was the present-day home of the Wilton Rancheria, a tribe that was nearly annihilated by white settlers in California during the 1800s.

The team were welcomed into the homes of a few families there to continue their planning and preparation to extract Raven and expose Biosmart.

When Carl arrived at the home where he was staying, he was happy to see Kendra and Lilly there. They hugged and kissed and finally Carl asked, "So you're in on this too?"

Kendra responded, "Yes, Lilly and I are here to take care of Raven once you guys free her. Remember, I'm a nurse."

"Are you going in the ambulance?" Carl asked.

"I don't know anything yet. They said we'd find out in a few days." Kendra responded.

"We'll find that out when we are supposed to know," Lilly said sternly.

They stayed up that night as their host family thanked them for what they are doing. The father of the family, John read a quote to Carl and Kendra from Doria Melliadis of the Iroquois that seemed to capture the spirit of cooperation that was involved in this movement.

*"Now they come to gather for the coming disaster and destruction of the white man by his own hands, with his own progressive, advanced, technological devices, that only the American Indian can avert. Now the time is near. And it is only the Indian who knows the cure. It is only the Indian who can stop this plague. And this time the invisible will be visible. And the unheard will be heard. And we will be seen, and we will be remembered."*

There was silence as they soaked in what John was saying. At that moment, Carl became that much more aware of what 'the cause' was all about. It was not just about freeing Lilly or everyone at Biosmart, but about freeing everyone from a life where technology dominates and controls humanity. Was this just the beginning?

They had a long talk that night about the kind of society they'd like to live in and how all this technology and surveillance was making it so much harder to achieve. They also talked about how outnumbered they were and wondered how many people would give up technology if they could. Kendra also wondered aloud if their dream was even possible outside of the native reservations and Damish communities.

Lilly then told them the story of the Pueblo Revolt in 1680 against the Spanish in northern New Mexico. In response to Spanish cruelty to the native Pueblo peoples, they rose up in revolt on the same day across the entire region, coordinated at a time before telephones or any technical means of communication. It took almost five years for 46 pueblos to be discreetly united on such a plan.

The leader of the uprising, Popé, sent out runners from Taos to all the pueblos carrying knotted cords to be untied each day and when the last knot was untied, the revolt was to begin. While the Spanish did capture two runners and found out about the plot, it was still a surprise at most sites. The ensuing uprising killed 400 Spanish occupiers and drove them out of the region for 12 years.

"In the same way," Lilly said "None of us are carrying a smartphone and we are not using any kind of traceable credit cards. We are making moves against the powerful outside of their view using the old ways, and we will surprise them."

### Endgame

For the next few weeks, they made preparations and rehearsed their plan at a nearby farm. They practiced moving quickly into the grounds behind the firetrucks in a tribal ambulance and learning tips from an EMT from the Wilton Rancheria so they would be more believable. After a few practice rounds, they asked him to be in the ambulance with Lilly, Kevin, and Carl, since he was a real EMT, leaving Kendra to wait at a nearby site where she would be waiting with nurses at the tribal health clinic to help Raven safely recover.

Finally, the night came for the extraction.

The crew drove down to Vallejo in staggered fashion and met up again at the Hunter Rest Area just outside of the city. There Lilly, Kevin, Carl, and Bruce the EMT mounted into the ambulance while Steve and two Damish from Colorado rode in the van. They had walkie talkies and earpieces so they could communicate, but only within half a mile so they had to stay close together.

They drove past all the refineries and stopped about six blocks away from Biosmart and waited for 10 o'clock when the hackers would set off the fire alarms. Carl's heart was pounding while Kevin, Lilly and Bruce the EMT seemed perfectly calm.

Once they heard the fire engine sirens at 10:05, they let them pass in front of them on the main road, then turned in behind them, with their warning lights on. As they sped the last few blocks, Carl saw the Biosmart facility gates open as the firetrucks passed through and he was surprised to see smoke coming from the grounds. Was there a real fire?

Little did Carl know but Steve and another team flew two drones over the facility and dropped smoke canisters from above to make the alarms more believable.

They pulled into the side of the building where they thought the brainworkers would be wheeled out and saw nothing. Did he drive to the wrong side?

Just then, a large door opened, and light came pouring out into the blackness of the night. Kevin, Lilly, and Bruce jumped out with a gurney and began wheeling it toward the building as workers were wheeling the first brainworkers out. Bruce tripped on something and turned his ankle, unable to run anymore. Carl then jumped out of the ambulance and helped Bruce hobble back and put him in the driver's seat.

"Can you drive?" Carl shouted.

"I think so," Bruce yelled. "And put on your mask!"

Carl put on his surgical mask then turned and ran into the light to help Lilly and Kevin look for Raven. He never wanted to ever set foot in the place again and here he was. He could feel his own heart beating out of his chest and tried to lengthen his breath in order to stay calm.

Inside it was chaos, with brainworkers being disconnected and various cables being thrown aside. Smoke also seemed to be inside the large room. *How did we do that? Or is it really on fire?* Carl thought.

Most of the technicians seemed to be focused on dismounting and securing the mainframe computer which held the AI, the real value of the place while a smaller team was dealing with the brainworkers.

Wearing medical face masks, Kevin and Lilly searched each row until they located Raven, who had already been unhooked from the system. They transferred her to the gurney and were wheeling her toward the door. A security guard tried to ask what they were doing so Kevin had to use his bossy surgeon presence to bully the guard, warning him that if they lost this brainworker, it would come out of his salary. The guard quickly backed off.

As Carl turned to run out behind them, he saw a gurney with a 20-something woman on it waiting to be wheeled outside. He got closer and saw a name tag that read "Nely." He pulled back her covers and saw the Tewa symbol tattooed on her shoulder. He then yelled, "I'll get this one" and rolled her out past the other brainworkers and over to the ambulance. In the chaos, no one even noticed.

One he got to the ambulance, Kevin had Raven inside where Lily was disabling her implants and looking after her. Once they saw Carl with another gurney they yelled, "we can't take more than one!"

"Oh yes we can!" Carl cried out. "I made a promise!"

Lilly shook her head in frustration, then grabbed a backboard and helped Carl move her onto it and strap her down. Since there was no room for two gurneys, they put her on the floor next to Raven's gurney and Bruce sped them out the gates with their emergency lights on and siren blaring.

Carl shined a powerful flashlight onto Nely's head where Lily made quick work of her implants once they were on the main road. Their adrenaline was surging and each of them expected to be chased down, so their eyes kept moving from their two patients to the back windows. Block after block they looked nervously, but no one followed.

Once the ambulance had left the gates Steve and his team attempted to enter and seize the backup drive, but they were unable to break into the small secure building without being detected. One member of Steve's team was able to enter the main building in the melee and managed to grab a laptop from one of the desks. They then radioed to a van parked about 100 meters away and quickly crawled back under the fence they had cut.

Once they were clear, they radioed again to the van and suddenly, all the lights at Biosmart went out. By then Steve and his team were back in their vehicle which had been parked a few hundred feet away and they sped back toward Wilton Rancheria.

Bruce's foot was aching so a few miles away, Carl took over driving duties again while Kevin and Lilly looked after Raven and Nely. Raven seemed stable but Nely was showing signs of shock.

It took over an hour to reach Sacramento after changing vehicles in Vacaville halfway there, putting Nely and Raven on stretchers in the back of a panel van at a rest area while someone else drove the ambulance back to where they had 'borrowed' it for a sizeable cash payment. The team then proceeded over to the tribal health clinic at Wilton Rancheria where Kendra and the other nurses were waiting.

Steve and his team rejoined them, and the entire group stayed up late that night with a mix of joy and relief, sitting around a fire behind a barn. They recounted what they had seen and done –and let their nerves slowly calm down. The tribal clinic also put Bruce in a soft cast, so he sat and made the others bring him beers from a big red cooler.

Never seeming to relax, Steve took notes on each of their stories and gave them all instructions to enjoy these moments tonight but to never discuss this night with anyone. People would be looking for them, but they'd left no digital traces. They should be safe so long as no one talks.

A few days later, Raven and Nely's parents arrived in Reno where they were reunited with their daughters while the rest of the team vanished.

Raven and her parents appeared on television one night in an exclusive feature on the abuses at Biosmart, even showing the fake death notice to the cameras and all the emails the company sent them claiming she was dead. She claimed to have been rescued by masked people that she was unable to clearly identify.

The FBI and California police soon descended on Vallejo and shut down Biosmart, arresting key officials and making them release the rest of the brainworkers. Work on their new facilities elsewhere ceased that week, Biosmart's stock plunged from $62 per share to less than 60 cent that weeks, a complete wipeout.

The police were also looking for the people who broke Raven and Nely out of Biosmart, but all leads turned out to be dead ends.

Nely's parents set out to drive her home to New Mexico and Rose put her right between them in the front seat of the truck. "I'm not a child!" Nely protested. Her mother only replied, "You're my child" and kept her arm around her all the way to the Las Vegas.

### Zipperhead, New Mexico

A few weeks later, Carl woke up next to Kendra at Zipperhead and heard a knock on the door. He opened the door and saw Steve standing in front of him with an envelope. He handed it to him saying, "Welcome to the rest of your life."

He could not help but laugh and said, "When will people stop saying that to me?"

Inside were all of his original documents as Carl Vigil. He also handed him a phone and said, "Its time you called your kids."

Carl turned to Kendra and was not sure who to call first. Since he saw Irene last, he decided to call Marco first. He texted to Irene that he would call in a while, and then dialed Marco.

"Hey son, how are you doing?" Carl said.

"Dad, oh my God is that you?" Marco yelled into the phone.

"Yeah, its me." Carl said.

"When are you coming home?" Marco asked.

"Right away Marco! I love you son," Carl said.

"I love you too Dad!" Marco cried.

Carl looked at Kendra and said, "Wanna go for a drive?"

"Yeah, but our work is far from done," she said.

"Indeed, its not!" Carl replied.

After that Carl called Irene for a teary phone reunion and made plans for his visit to see them all in California. The last thing he said to her was, "You saved my life."

### Sunnyvale, California

The next week, Nichelle arrived at the benefactor's office at his company headquarters in to report on how well his money had been spent. Once she completed her briefing, he seemed very pleased.

"Excellent! So they are out of business, and we have their technology. Now the market is ours for the taking," he said.

*"Upon suffering beyond suffering, the Red Nation shall rise again, and it shall be a blessing for a sick world.*

*A world filled with broken promises, selfishness and separations. A world longing for light again. I see a time of seven generations when all the colors of mankind will gather under the sacred Tree of Life and the whole Earth will become one circle again.*

*In that day there will be those among the Lakota who will carry knowledge and understanding of unity among all living things and the young white ones will come to those of my people and ask for wisdom.*

*I salute the light within your eyes where the whole universe dwells. For when you are at that center within you and I am in that place within me, we shall be as one."*

~ *Crazy Horse, Chief of the* Oglala band of Lakota Sioux

## CHAPTER FOUR

# FASTER

**M**uncie, Indiana

A grey sky hung over the town full of red brick and clapboard houses. The tidy streets stood out in a landscape of frozen grass and leafless trees. Inside the high school, shouts echoed from inside the natatorium.

The thick black line passing under him, Doug's arms churned in the water as his mind wandered between how he would finish his essay that was due tomorrow and whether he should ask out Sabine, the new girl from Colorado. Was he reading the signals right or was she just being polite? He had no idea.

Soon the blue wall appeared, and he dropped his shoulder into a flip turn, something he must have done thousands of times. He planted his feet firmly right on the center of the black tile cross on the wall and pushed off, dolphin kicking out past the flags before picking up his freestyle stroke again. *"Yeah, maybe I'll just ask her out,"* he thought.

*"Dad always said that you've got to take risks if you want to achieve anything in this life,"* he pondered. These thoughts continued as he cranked through an interval set of 5 x 300 yards while his coach yelled at the younger swimmers two lanes down for loafing.

Doug always thought he could write books with the thoughts he had during swim practice, if only he had a way to write them down. During the cool down Doug started dreaming of cheeseburgers and wondering what his Mom was making for dinner that night. Whatever it was, he would eat it all and probably still be hungry.

Once practice ended, he and the others put away their kickboards and pull buoys and went to the showers. They were all too tired to get rowdy or bully the freshman tonight since Coach Getz had been loading up their workouts the last few weeks before starting to taper them off for the sectional and state meets.

Charles "Chuck" Getz stood at the edge of the pool, arms crossed, eyes scanning the water with the same measured intensity that once dissected crime scenes. His face, weathered by years of late nights and early mornings, bore the faint lines of a man who had seen more than he cared to remember. He had the build of a man who had known strength, but now it was the kind that came more from resolve than from muscle. His years as a detective left him with a certain stillness, a way of standing that conveyed both patience and readiness, as if he were always waiting for something, always expecting the unexpected. This always came in very handy when dealing with high school boys.

All Doug could think about was food since swim practice always left him ravenous.

He blasted through the door in his usual fashion, throwing his bag of wet swim gear by the door, taking off his winter coat, and heading into the kitchen. The wooden floors creaked beneath his feet and a subtle cloud of chlorinated air seemed to travel with him through the house.

He was a boy on the cusp of something, though what that was remained unclear, even to him. His lanky frame bore the telltale signs of potential yet to be fulfilled, muscles half-formed beneath a layer of adolescent softness.

His hair, perpetually damp and tousled, clung to his forehead in a way that suggested he'd long given up trying to tame it. The smell of chlorine clung to him, mingling with the faint scent of sweat and something else, something unnameable, that always seemed to hover around boys like him—those caught in the space between boyhood and the first stirrings of manhood.

"Is your hair still wet?" his mother asked as she peered at him with her forest green eyes, her gaze both unsettling and mesmerizing. She could scold with a question or even a glance and he could not remember a moment that she had ever raised her voice.

He could never lie to her and when she looked at him, it was as though she was seeing into the very core of his being. Her presence was a quiet storm wrapped in grace.

"Yeah Mom," Doug said sheepishly. And without another word from her he went upstairs to dry his hair.

On his way back down the moment he passed by the front door she called out, "Where are your wet things?"

"*How does she always know*?" he thought to himself.

"Is Dad eating with us tonight?" he asked as he plopped down on a stool in the kitchen.

"No honey, he has band practice again," she said, referring to the rock band that seemed to consume her husband Jeff's evenings the past year.

"OK, so what are we eating?" Doug inquired, not seeing any food being prepared.

"I had a long day at work, so I ordered us pizza," his mother said.

"Please tell me you got more than one!" He asked longingly.

"Of course, silly!" She replied. "Feeding you is like feeding two kids!"

Doug munched on a half-eaten bag of nacho chips he found on the counter and waited for the doorbell to ring so he could finally feed his starving body. Finally, the doorbell rang, and Doug sprinted to the door and returned to the kitchen with two large pizza boxes and laid them out on the table.

By the time his mother got to the table, Doug was on his second piece. She grimaced and said, "I swear, sometimes it's like I'm raising a wolf."

Not looking up he mumbled "sorry" through a mouthful of pizza. She gently put her hair into a ponytail then picked up some plates and knives to bring to the table. She ended up sitting next to him since his flipped open pizza box left no room to eat at the seat across from him. She put a plate and fork next to him and gave him a glance that made him pull a piece onto it instead of wolfing it straight from the box. He also shifted and sat up straight.

She rolled her eyes and thought to herself, *"I am not going to raise an uncivilized baboon if I can help it."* She then pulled a piece of pizza from the other box onto her plate and began to eat.

The contrast between them was both typical and striking at the same time. Her long raven colored hair and red tunic sweater and leggings was sharp contrast to his shock of chlorine-bleached hair and warmups.

Later close to 9 o'clock, Jeff arrived carrying an electric guitar case and asked, "Hey, did you save me dinner?

Jeff was a man of dual natures, a polymath with a rebel's heart, his life a seamless blend of intellect and passion, each feeding the other in a harmony only he could create.

"I sure did, and you're lucky our son did not devour it all," Joanne replied from the living room where she was working on a crochet project while watching a movie. "There is most of a pizza in the oven," she added.

"So that's where you were hiding it," Doug impishly said.

"Don't even think about it," Jeff said as he put down his guitar case, hung up his coat, and took off his wet shoes. "Looks like It started snowing again," he said.

"Our strong well-fed son can take care of that in the morning!" Joanne laughed.

"Oh mom, seriously?" Doug said. "I already have to be up at five to get to practice."

"It only takes you 10 minutes and it's not like we're charging you rent," she smiled.

"Listen to your mother," Jeff called out from the kitchen. "Do you have any homework tonight?" he asked.

"Ugh," Doug said, and he went upstairs to his room, presumably to do his homework. They were never quite sure until grades were posted but they seldom had to worry.

The next weekend was the big meet for the Olympic Conference, a collection of high schools in central Indiana and their final big competition before sectionals and the state championship. Doug's team, the Muncie Northside Titans, were expected to do well and challenge the regional powerhouses from Allisonville and Rangeline High Schools.

Doug was among the top swimmers in Indiana at the 200- and 500-yard freestyle and he finished third the conference and sixth at state last year as a sophomore, seven seconds ahead of his arch-rival from Rangeline, Conor Nelson. The first and second place conference finishers from the previous year both graduated and got swimming scholarships at Auburn and Stanford so this should be Doug's year.

While Doug was not a bad student, his main focus was on swimming faster. He lived and breathed the sport. All his friends were swimmers, and he even spent summers working as a lifeguard and training at the nearby Catalina Club. If he competed in any sport on land he would be called a gym rat.

Chuck did not plan to taper his Northside Titans' workouts for this meet, so the intensity was not reduced to allow them to swim their best times just yet. Instead, they powered through their grueling intervals all week. Their coach wanted them to be peaking during sectionals and beyond, but that was still three weeks away. Once this weekend meet was over, the taper would begin.

The team all boarded the bus early on Saturday morning for the ride to Kokomo Haworth high school where the Olympic conference championships were being held. Their parents and friends were driving over in cars, and most would ride home with their parents afterwards.

The cacophony of a high school swim meet is not unlike the sound of a zoo at feeding time with shouts and grunts echoing off the walls of the natatorium. For a big meet like this one, you could already start hearing the sounds from the frozen parking lot. Parents gingerly walked on the icy pavement, making clouds with their warm breath in the frigid air as they tried not to slip on any patches of ice.

Soon the starting official's rhythm of 'take your mark...bee p" made the shouts and cheering from inside to became even more intense. The first shock came when Muncie Northside's heavily favored 200 medley relay team finished second behind Rangeline. Their swimmers seemed to be posting their best times of the year, and not by small margins. Everyone knew they had been improving, but not like this.

Doug was stoked for the 200-yard freestyle and when the race started, he eyed Connor Nelson in lane 3 next to him and felt confident. Swimming in lane 4, his long and steady strokes had him tied for the lead through the first 100 yards. But after the turn for the second half of the race, Connor started to pull away by a body length. Doug at first wanted to overtake him right away but he remembered his coach's instructions on pacing and to "swim his race." Nonetheless, he could not help but pick up the pace and try to stay close to Conor in the lead.

By the time they hit the wall for the final 25 yards, Connor was almost three body lengths ahead and a swimmer from Allisonville in lane 2 was even with Doug. *"How could this be happening?"* he thought.

Connor Nelson of Rangeline ended up winning the race a full six seconds ahead of Doug, who ended up third behind a sophomore from Allisonville who just touched him out for second.

As they pulled their soaked and exhausted bodies from the pool, Doug put on a good face but inside he was shocked since he finished exactly where he did in last year's conference meet. He congratulated Connor and the swimmer from Allisonville then went back to down an energy drink so he can get ready for the 500-yard freestyle later.

Coach Getz sought to console Doug, telling him, "These guys have got to be tapered already. Don't worry, you'll get them at state when you are too."

This seemed to at least partially calm Doug's nerves, but he still did not like getting beaten like that. Not one bit.

Tom, one of the seniors sitting on the bench near Doug put on his swim cap, stood up, and started to unwind his shoulders for the 100 breaststroke which was coming up soon.

"Hey man," he said. "My cousin over there swims for Rangeline and he said they haven't even started to taper yet."

"No way!" Doug said. "But what if he is just bullshitting and messing with us?"

Tom replied, "Well, we'll find out soon enough. Wish me luck," he then grabbed his goggles and walked off toward the starting blocks.

"Good luck man – you've got this" Doug urged.

The rest of the meet continued to provide shocking results as a few swimmers from Rangeline and Allisonville seemed to be throwing down incredible times in each event. Doug was already less than 100% after putting so much into the 200 but his 500 result was similar, finishing second behind Connor Nelson again. What was going on?

By the time the culminating 400-yard freestyle relay had begun, the crowd was abuzz about how fast Connor Nelson and the other two swimmers were this year. Connor had been rising star last year, but the other two seemed to have come out of nowhere.

After the meet, Chuck talked to Steve Johnson, the Rangeline coach, and asked how they were getting such great results. They both said they were not doing anything different this year, but that a few of their kids just seemed to be blooming this year. Chuck had his doubts but given how close the swim coaching community was, he did not want to say anything until he looked into it himself.

One of the other team's coaches walked past with a look of disgust on his face, saying the word "doping" under his breath as he passed them.

On the drive home, the normally gregarious Doug was silent most of the way as he sat next to his wet gym bag in the back seat. His mother

Joanne kept trying to cheer him up, but it only seemed to make him feel worse. He felt humiliated and started to wonder if maybe he had not pushed himself hard enough in training all year.

Finally, he spoke up. "Dad, am I lazy?'

Jeff turned from the driver's seat and took a quick glance at his son before putting his eyes back on the graying snow blown road.

He adjusted his glasses and asked, "Do you mean swimming or life in general?"

Joanne quickly punched her husband in the shoulder to scold him, saying, "No honey, no one is more dedicated to swimming than you are."

"Your mom's right," Jeff said. "You punish yourself in the pool and weight room and I don't know anyone who would call you lazy, unless it's helping around the house."

This made Doug crack just a hint of a smile, "Ah c'mon, I'm not that bad, am I?"

"I'll let your mother answer that," Jeff said with an impish grin in Joanne's direction.

She quickly deflected saying, "Do we want to stop and eat on the way home?"

Both Jeff and Doug almost shouted, "Yes!" Joanne allowed herself a subtle smirk, knowing that food was always the way into their hearts.

Muncie Northside was in a different sectional than most of the schools in their conference and Doug was able to win the 200- and 500-yard freestyle to qualify for the state meet. Their team finished second in the sectional overall with Richmond placing first. Northside also managed to send six swimmers to the state meet in Indianapolis the following week.

Doug and his teammates went online that night to see how their main competition fared in their sectionals and were floored. Connor

Nelson set state records in the 200- and 500-yard freestyle while one other Rangeline swimmer and one Allisonville swimmer all posted times that would seed them very high next week in Indianapolis. A few of them were just average swimmers last year so how was this even possible?

The next Monday before practice, Doug came in early and asked his coach what he thought was happening.

"Coach, do you think they're doping?" he asked.

"I don't know and it's not an accusation we can be throwing out there. There is a drug test at State, so they'll find out if that is the case," Chuck responded.

He continued, "The main thing for all of you guys is to stay focused on your training this week, get lots of sleep, and don't get sick. Hell, wear a mask at school if you want to make sure."

"OK coach," Doug replied but his body language did not indicate that he was convinced this was the end of the story.

The ever-observant Coach Getz, picked up on this and reassured Doug, "If there is anything weird happening, I'll find out. Until then, keep doing your best. It's all we can do right now."

Doug nodded and twisted his face a bit, then walked off to change for practice.

The following week at the Indiana high school swimming championships in Indianapolis, the same swimmers from Rangeline and Allisonville set new state records and trounced the field in their events. Some of their performances would have even placed them well at the collegiate level. Thankfully, none of them competed in the backstroke or butterfly events.

Doug finished fourth in the 200-yard freestyle and third in the 500. While it was not a bad outing, it was a disappointment since he expected to be on top of the podium in at least one event this year.

Jeff and Joane talked to Chuck after the meet and asked him what he thought was going on with these swimmers.

"My son seems to train with monastic dedication so I can't seem to believe these kids are working that much harder than he is," Jeff said.

"Yeah, he is our team workhorse, but there may be other factors too since some kids blossom at different ages," Chuck replied.

"But these few kids seemed to burst out of nowhere and now they're way faster than the others. How can that be? Do you think they're doping?" Joanne asked.

"It's hard to say but I have my own suspicions which I am checking out right now," Chuck said.

"Oh that's right, you used to be a cop. How did you end up being a swim coach?" Joanne laughed since she knew the answer already.

"A detective baby," Jeff interjected, drawing a slight frown on Joanne's face.

"Well, I was a swimmer myself and when my son Jacob started swimming, I got into coaching since I did not see anyone around who seemed to know what they were doing," Chuck said with a wry smile.

"So, can you find out what may be happening with these Rangeline and Allisonville kids?" Jeff asked.

"Look, I'm not going to go snooping around myself, but I do have a few feelers out with another private detective here in Indy. They owe me a favor so let me see what they can find out", Chuck said.

"OK, thanks" Joanne beamed.

"And please don't tell anyone, especially not the kids. It would be bad for my business if this got out. Plus, it would make it harder for us to find out if anything strange is happening," Chuck instructed them.

Joanne nodded that she understood.

"So, they'd cover their tracks?" Jeff asked.

"Bingo," Getz replied, then asked, "Are you guys staying in Indy tonight?"

"Yeah, we got a room downtown and tickets to see the Pacers. Doug loves Tyrese Halliburton." Joanne replied.

"Who doesn't?" Chuck said. "Back-to-back NBA championships will do that."

A short time later Doug came out of the locker room with wet hair and dressed in his blue Northside swimming warmups. It was always a bit funny how similar Doug and his father looked at times like this. They had many of the same mannerisms and even dressed in the same sporty clothing, the only exception being that Jeff usually had a band t-shirt of some kind on under his layers.

Joanne on the other hand refused to "dress like a slob" even for a day in a big sweaty natatorium. Her red knit dress, leggings, big gold earrings, and knee-high boots indicated a level of style and dignity that she would never let go of. Her clothes seemed less an outfit and more an extension of her being, each piece worn not with ostentation but with a subtlety that whispered of refinement.

There was a certain economy in her movements, a grace that suggested she had long ago mastered the art of making everything look effortless.

To see her was to understand that style was not a thing one could buy; it was something that emanated from within, a quiet, unassuming power that left its mark on everyone she encountered.

Joanne asked, "Where is your coat? Its freezing outside!"

Looking startled, Doug said "Oh" and ran back into the locker room, presumably to fetch his coat.

He appeared a short time later with his coat on and they all found their way to the parking garage. That night they went to Gainbridge fieldhouse to see the Pacers barely beat the Phoenix Suns after watching Doug eat two big burgers at a nearby sports bar called the Yard House.

Joanne, a vegetarian, had tucked out to at a vegan place next door called the Electric Goddess. She had to plan these trips for them carefully lest she never get a chance to eat.

February in central Indiana can look like a frozen tundra of gray leafless trees and frozen grass but a new blanket of snow fell as Jeff and Joanne now pressed Doug to catch up on his schoolwork. He had neglected a few assignments during the late swim season, so he had a lot of catching up to do. One of his teachers, Mrs. Dezelan, was kind enough to give him an extension on a paper due to his swimming commitments.

"You can't get a swim scholarship if you don't have the grades," Jeff constantly told him so often that Doug would even mockingly mouth the words.

"Hey, did you ever ask out Sabine?" Jeff asked his son.

The first week of March, Chuck called Jeff to arrange to have coffee with he and Joanne at a place near the Ball State campus. He asked them to leave Doug at home and not to tell him anything, yet. They had a feeling they knew what it was about but could not be quite sure. Was a college interested in Doug or did he find out what was going on with these new super swimmers?

They met for a late breakfast at a place called the Sunshine Cafe, not far from Northside high school. Jeff worked remotely so he had no trouble getting off work but Joanne, a psychologist, had to rearrange a few of her appointments to make it.

Chuck greeted them and they all sat at a quiet booth in one corner. After exchanging pleasantries and ordering their food, Chuck finally told them why he wanted to see them this morning.

"So, what do you know about genetic engineering?" Chuck asked them.

"What?" Joanne replied.

"In what sense?" Jeff said. "I mean, you read about it now and then as a treatment for diseases."

"Yes, but now it's being tested for other things too, like human performance," Chuck deadpanned.

"Oh my God, is that what they are doing?" Joanne asked. "Is that how those kids got so much faster?

"I think so," Chuck replied.

"OK, what can you tell us?" Jeff asked.

"According to my colleague in Indy, Cillairne, you know, the big biotech and pharmaceutical company there has been working on gene editing for human performance," Chuck said.

He continued, "And one way they've spent a lot of money on the last few years is a method to improve lactate metabolism."

"What does that do?" Jeff asked.

"You mean lactate like lactic acid or lactation like breast feeding?" Joanne asked.

"I mean lactic acid metabolism," Chuck replied. "You know how Michael Phelps was known for having a body that did not produce much lactic acid?"

"Oh yeah, and he could train longer and hard than anyone else. He also did not wear out in races like the others," Jeff said.

"Exactly," Chuck nodded.

Just then, a waitress appeared with a cart full of steaming plates of eggs and toast. She placed their orders in front of them, refilled their coffee, and left.

"So, they've figured out how to make kids into Michael Phelps?" Joanne asked.

"Yes and no," Chuck replied. "They don't know how to make a body produce less lactic acid, but they do have an experimental way to make people metabolize it much faster which leads to almost the same effect."

"Holy shit," Jeff said, then dug into his breakfast.

"So how do we know these kids are having their genes edited?" Joanne asked.

Chuck replied, "What I have is circumstantial, but I think its correct. Connor Nelson's Dad is the senior director for new product development at Cillairne."

"Oh damn," Jeff said. "So he us using his own kid as a guinea pig?"

"Maybe, unless they are so far along that they think its safe now" Chuck replied.

Joanne twisted her crimson lips and asked, "so how would that explain the other kids?"

"The other one lives on the same street in Rangeline as Connor Nelson." Chuck replied. "So there is a good chance their parents are friends or at least the kids are."

Jeff looked up from his plate and asked "And the kid from Allisonville? How are they getting this too?"

Chuck paused for a moment before replying, "I'm not sure yet but I think they may have a connection to Cillairne as well."

They all sat in silence for a moment to soak it all in before Joanne spoke up.

"Do you think their coaches know?' she asked.

"It's hard to say," Getz replied. "I've known Steve Johnson for years and I'd have a hard time thinking he would lie to me."

"Can't they get caught through testing?" Jeff asked.

"I don't think so since there is no way to test for it and right now, technically, it's not against state rules, yet," Chuck responded.

"I wonder how safe any of this is in the long run," Joanne pondered.

"Yeah, me too," Chuck said.

"Well, they must be doing this under a doctor's supervision," Jeff said. "I used to work in medical sales, and I got to see how they do medical trials on all kinds of things."

"Maybe you can find out who that doctor is?" Joanne asked.

"My friend in Indy is working on that," Chuck replied.

"Jeez, once word of this kind of thing get out, every kid will want this – including our own son," Jeff said and glanced at Joanne.

Joanne looked down and shook her head.

"So, what do we tell our son?" she asked.

"For now, nothing," Chuck said. "None of these kids can keep a secret and we need to learn a lot more ourselves before we tell them anything."

"Fair enough," Jeff said.

About a week later, by which time the snow had turned to brown slush, Chuck invited Jeff and Joanne over to play cards with him and his wife Linda, the drama teacher at Northside.

Chuck fell in love with Linda after swearing he'd never get married again. To him, she was the embodiment of unspent youth, and her golden hair caught light as if the sun itself conspired to crown her with an eternal summer. She moved with a lightness that suggested she carried no burdens, only the joy of possibility and the thrill of a yet-to-be performed scene.

Joanne liked Linda a lot, especially since she was not one-dimensional and liked to talk about things other than swimming or the price of cheese. Chuck and Linda Getz were fun hosts. Their frequent and unrestrained laughter filled the room with the kind of warmth that made you believe, if only for a moment, that life was a thing to be embraced, not merely endured.

Joanne and Jeff stomped the slush off their boots and came inside to the smell of a crackling fire and warm drinks. After a few rounds of cards, the topic eventually tuned to swimming and genetic engineering.

"So, a bit of news," Chuck said and sighed.

"So, you know too?" Joanne asked Linda, who nodded.

"The Allisonville swimmer does have a parent who works at Cillairne under Connor Nelson's dad," Chuck said.

"So there is the connection," Jeff said.

"What about the doctor?" Joanne asked.

"Oof, here we go now," Linda added.

"We think the doctor monitoring all of this is one at the IU Med Center in Indy who does grant work for Cillairne," Chuck said. "So far as we can tell, he has been seeing these boys since last spring so that may be how long they have been undergoing this gene editing treatment."

"And just look at the results," Jeff said.

"I can't help but think all of this will go wrong at some point," Linda added. "I mean, they are experimenting with these young boys' bodies while they are still developing. Who knows what could happen?"

"I agree, and I can't imagine if Doug wanted to do this." Joanne said.

"Oh, you know he will," Jeff said.

"I don't doubt that either," Chuck added.

"So, what do we do here?" Joanne asked.

"I think I need to find a time to sit down with Steve Johnson and see how much he really knows, then go from there" Chuck said.

"Like you said, they aren't technically breaking any rules." Jeff opined.

"I mean, what about the bigger questions here?" Linda asked. "This can't be cheap so now the richer kids get even more advantages?"

Joanne jumped in, "And the best swimming scholarships will go to the kids who don't even need them? Is this where we're going?"

"Isn't it kinda like that now?" Chuck asked. "The families who can afford the age group swim clubs, travel meets, and summer swim camps have a leg up already don't they?"

"But this is different," Linda said. "This is buying human ability. What next, gene editing for higher SAT scores? Isn't our society unequal enough already?"

Joanne let out an exasperated breath.

Jeff added, "It's like we're regressing into feudal times again. Whatever happened to equality in our society?"

"Oh, that ship sailed a long time ago," Linda said.

Chuck left the room and returned with a bottle of Irish whiskey and said, "I think we all need a drink."

Two weeks later, Chuck called Jeff to talk about his chat with Rangeline coach Steve Johnson. As Chuck described it, it took him awhile to get Johnson to finally admit that he knew that two of his swimmers were part of an advanced medical trial.

"What was I supposed to do Chuck, I can't say no to these rich parents, or they'll destroy me," Johnson said during his discussion with Chuck.

"No man, I get it – especially in your school district," Chuck consoled him.

It turns out that Steve Johnson had also been made part of the data gathering effort by providing metabolic measurements after each week under the cover of doing it for the entire team to measure their progress. It also did not hurt that he was paid a monthly fee for the role, something a person on a public-school teacher's salary always needed.

Johnson also claimed that everything he saw so far told him the entire procedure was safe and had no bad side effects, except they needed a lot more rest after being able to push themselves so hard.

Chuck promised not to report any of this to state swimming officials, but he also wanted one or two of his swimmers to be given a chance to be part of the same medical trial. Chuck told Jeff that Johnson had his doubts the Muncie kids could even afford it, and that Chuck had told him not to be so sure about that.

"Nonetheless, I got you and Doug a meeting next Wednesday down at the IU Medical Center, if you want it," Chuck said.

"Oh man, I don't know how I feel about this, and I know Joanne will hate the idea," Jeff said.

"It's just a meeting and some blood tests and such on Doug," Chuck replied. "He may not even medically qualify for the trial."

"And what about the cost?" Jeff asked.

"They can tell you that but I'm guessing the price is very steep," Chuck said.

"Like how steep," Jeff asked.

"Like probably north of $50,000," Chuck said.

"OK, I need to talk to Joanne and Doug about this," Jeff said.

That night Doug was out seeing a movie with friends, so Jeff told Joanne what he'd learned from Chuck that day.

"Are you kidding me?" She said. "Why are you even considering this?"

"Because I love my son and I want him to succeed," Jeff replied. "Plus, it's just a meeting to talk about it, get some tests, and see if it's something to consider."

"I love him too and I don't want him to get sick or anything. I also don't want him to think he can just take shortcuts in life" Joanne said.

"And don't just tell me this will cost nothing," Joanne scolded. Now she was getting angry.

Jeff paused, which told her everything. She glared and waited for an answer.

"It may cost a lot, but isn't that why we saved so much for so long?" Jeff asked.

"Why even try to get a scholarship if we just going to throw away his college money so he can swim seven seconds faster." Joanne said in a raised voice, something she seldom ever did.

"My love," Jeff said, "Doug is better at this than I've ever been at anything in my life. He could even be an Olympian someday. Don't you want that for him?"

"Of course I do," she said. "I just don't want to turn my precious boy into Frankenstein," she replied in tears.

"It's just a meeting to learn more, that's it," Jeff said.

"But you know he'll be excited and want to do it," she replied.

"Don't sell our son short, he may seem like an airhead but there is real substance in there Joanne," Jeff said.

"Our son is not a bully, and he sticks up for the kids who are bullied," Jeff said. "He helps out the neighbors and shovels the snow from old Mrs. Duchane's driveway without being asked, even if he bitches about doing ours."

"Well, I have raised him right," Joanne said, wiping he tears away.

"He's a good kid and you know it." Jeff said. "Let's see if he has the character we think he does."

"You really are good at this sales stuff," Joanne said. "OK, but I'm only agreeing to the meeting and tests, but anything beyond that means a separate family decision. He's my kid and it's my money too"

"Absolutely, my love," Jeff said and embraced her on the sofa. They hugged for a long time, and she said, "I hope you know what you're doing."

"Me too," Jeff replied.

That night Doug came home from the movies, and they decided not to tell him until Friday night or Saturday morning. They did not want him to be tempted to tell everyone at school.

It turned out that Doug did ask Sabine out over a week ago and she also went along with his friends to the movie on Wednesday night. Joanne felt bad that her mother's intuition did not pick up on her son suddenly having a new love interest. Was she losing her touch?

They could not tell Doug about the new developments on Friday night since he also had a date with Sabine that night to see a new movie about zombie mutants. Like so many teenage boys who took their dates to scary films, Doug was hoping she would get scared and move closer to cuddle him.

Saturday morning, Jeff made blueberry pancakes while Joanne drank her coffee and read a hardback book. They both waited for their son to wake up, something which happened a lot later now that swim season was over.

Doug finally rumbled down the stairs at about 10:30 which cued Jeff to turn on the griddle again.

"Good morning dear," Joanne greeted her son from her reading chair.

"Something smells good," he replied as he wiped the sleep from his green eyes.

"Come on in here, we've got pancakes." Jeff said

They all sat down together at the kitchen table, Joanne with her coffee and Doug eagerly awaiting a stack of pancakes.

Jeff was standing at the griddle dressed in a blue bathrobe with a Dinosaur Jr t-shirt on underneath it and holding a spatula. "Coming right up!" he announced.

"So, how did it go with Sabine?" Joanne asked her son.

Doug buried his head in his hands and said "ugh."

"That bad?" she asked.

"Maybe worse," Doug replied.

Two minutes later, Jeff placed a big plate of pancakes in from of Doug and watched him attack it with vigor. Joanne cleared her throat gently, which triggered Doug to sit up straight and eat less like a wild animal. Jeff and Joanne looked at each other and gently laughed.

Once Doug finished off his plate, his mother told him to clean it off in the sink and to bring her the pot of coffee. They then refilled their coffee mugs and Jeff said, "We have some news for you."

"Wait, are you guys getting divorced?" He asked.

"No silly, your Dad can't do better than me," Joanne cackled.

"That's true," Jeff added.

"I'm going to be a big brother?" He asked. "Mom, you're not even showing."

Joanne mimed slapping her son and said, "Wrong again."

"We know why Connor and the other two go so fast," Jeff deadpanned and took a sip of coffee.

"No way, how?" Doug asked, leaning forward on the table.

"Do you remember what made Michael Phelps so fast?" his mother asked.

"His huge wingspan?" Doug guessed.

"What else?" Joanne asked him.

"Oh yeah, he didn't even feel the lactic acid burn," Doug said.

"His body did not produce the normal amount of lactic acid so he would train longer and harder. He could also go at a faster pace before the lactic acid burn would wear him out," Jeff said.

"So they found a way to do that?" Doug asked.

"Sort of," Joanne said.

"They found a way to make them metabolize lactic acid faster so it's almost the same effect," Jeff replied.

"Damn, no wonder he pulled away like that in the 200 and 500," Doug sighed.

"So they broke the rules, we need to report them!" Doug said excitedly.

"Not exactly, since technically it's not against the rules yet and there is no way to test for it," Jeff said.

"Oooh," Doug replied.

"And there may be a way for you to do it too," Jeff said.

"Don't say it like that!" Joanne said. "Dear, we still don't know much about this or how safe it is, but some people want to meet with you and talk about it."

"Really? When?" he asked.

"I'm taking you out of school on Wednesday and we're going to Indy for a doctor's appointment" Jeff said.

"Is Mom coming too?" Doug asked.

"I can't dear, I have a full schedule." Joanne replied. "But no decisions will be made this week, you're just going to learn about what it entails and have some tests done to see if you even qualify."

"OK, sounds cool," Doug said. "Is anyone using the TV now? I wanna play some Xbox."

"No buddy, and before you go, one more thing. Don't tell anyone. I mean anyone about this," Jeff said.

"Why not?" he asked. "If we're not doing anything wrong, then why be worried?"

"Dear, it's because we still aren't sure what all of this is or what it even means. We're in a learning phase and its best to do that privately," Joanne urged.

"OK Mom, that makes sense," Doug replied then ran off to start gaming while big fluffy flakes of snow fell outside.

Jeff and Joanne looked at each other a bit surprised.

Jeff said, "I thought he would be all excited, but he seems pretty levelheaded about it."

"Let's see if he stays that way, Joanne said, then kissed her husband and went back to her reading chair. Jeff went upstairs to his office to pull out his Fender Jaguar guitar and start playing some new cover songs his band was working on.

The following Wednesday, Jeff and Doug scraped the ice from the windshield of the car and drove down I-69 toward Indianapolis. Doug was not allowed to eat any breakfast since he had to be fasting prior to the blood tests that morning. The whole drive down he hoped he could do the lab tests first since he was starving.

They pulled into one of the parking garages at the IU Medical Center downtown and Jeff turned to his son and asked, "Are you ready for this?"

Doug answered, "Oh yeah."

The followed several signs over to the IU Medical School then up to Research section and found the office of Dr Timothy Joseph, a tall man with natural charm and charisma. He was not exactly the type of person you expected to find running medical trials. He had an informal air about him, the kind of guy who would be happy eating pizza from the box and not from a plate. He insisted on being called Tim.

Once they sat down, Doug looked at all the certificates and diplomas on Dr. Tim's wall. Medical diplomas, varsity awards from North Carolina State, and even a high school All-American swimming certificate for the 100-yard backstroke.

Doug blurted out, "Wow, All-American! So, you were a swimmer, too?"

"I still am if you count Masters," Tim chuckled. "Yeah, I used to be pretty fast and now I'm just happy to keep going. I heard you're pretty fast yourself."

"He sure is and I'm hoping you can tell us a bit about how he can get even faster," Jeff said.

"Hold on now, there is a lot to unpackage here," Tim said.

Doug sat up straight and listened as the doctor explained the whole process while his father took notes.

"Lactic acid accumulates in the muscles, leading to an increase in hydrogen ions, which lowers the pH within the muscle cells - making them more acidic," Dr Tim explained. "This acidification can interfere with the enzymes responsible for energy production and muscle contraction, leading to muscle fatigue and a decreased in performance." He checked to see if Doug and Jeff were following along and so far, they were so he continued.

"What we are trying to learn is how we can increase the body's ability to metabolize this lactic acid by producing more of the enzymes that break it down," Dr Tim said.

"And if you do that, you can swim faster and longer without getting tired?" Doug inquired.

"Precisely," Dr Tim said. "There is other research being done to reduce a protein called myostatin, which inhibits muscle growth so that muscles can grow even larger and stronger. But that is more of something for weightlifters and football players."

"Wow," Jeff said. "It's like steroids."

"And without the 'roid rage," Dr Tim added.

Doug was still soaking it all in.

"But in your case Doug, we don't want to reduce lactic acid too much since your body still needs it to stimulate adaptations in your body so there is still a bit of burn, but not quite as much." Dr Tim added.

"So how is this even done?" Jeff asked.

Dr Tim took off his glasses and looked them both in the eye.

"First off, it's all a very carefully orchestrated process, blending advanced science with meticulous precision. First, we do a thorough consultation which we can start today with a number of tests that will be examined by geneticists and doctors. Then, if we think it's safe, we'll talk with you and your parents to ensure everyone understands the goals, risks, and potential outcomes. Do you understand everything so far?" He asked.

They both nodded yes, then Dr Tim stood up and continued to speak while drawing diagrams on a dry erase board.

"We use a technique called CRISPR-Cas9. In this process, the Cas9 protein, guided by a specially designed RNA sequence, is introduced into your cells, either through an injection or via a viral vector engineered to deliver the necessary genetic tools."

"Like a virus?" Doug asked.

"Yes, but it's one that we've designed," Dr Tim responded as he motioned to his drawing on the board. He continued.

"The Cas9 acts like molecular scissors, cutting the DNA at the precise location of the target gene. Once the DNA is cut, your cell's natural repair mechanisms take over with what we put in there. In your case, we'll introduce a new piece of DNA to increase the production of the correct enzyme, so you'll process lactic acid even faster," Dr Tim concluded. "From the introduction of the new DNA sequence to feeling the effects can take hours, days, and sometimes even weeks."

"OK, so is that done in a single visit or something?" Jeff asked.

Dr Tim shook his head as if to say "no."

"The whole process is performed in a highly controlled environment, and Doug would need to be monitored closely for any immediate reactions or side effects. So, we plan on one week here at the hospital," Dr Tim responded.

"And what about after that?" Doug asked.

"I'm glad you asked that Doug," Dr Tim said. "Over the following weeks and months, we'd need to track how your body responds to the edited genes and look for signs of successful integration and any unintended consequences."

"Unintended consequences?" Jeff asked. "Like what?"

"OK, first off, if we see any signs in your blood work or DNA that it's not safe for you, then we don't do it. No way," Dr Tim explained. "But nothing is guaranteed 100%, even though we do everything to keep it safe," Dr Tim said.

"So what could happen?" Doug asked

"We've never had any problems yet with the others in the trial but the things we check for afterwards include checking your general health and seeing if you have any allergic reactions; blood tests to check other reactions and to measure the expression of the targeted gene to ensure that the editing has taken place and is functioning as intended," Dr Tim said.

"We also may do imaging studies to visualize any internal changes or to assess if the gene editing has impacted any unintended areas. Then of course we do genetic sequencing on cells from key muscles to help identify any off-target effects or unintended genetic modifications." Tim explained.

"Wow, that's a lot," Doug said.

"Well, there is more," Dr Tim said. "Over the long term, you'll need to be monitored for any late-onset side effects, such as inflammation or abnormal cell growth. We'll also need to do regular assessments of your immune system to make sure your body is not mounting an immune response against the edited cells or the gene-editing tools." Dr Tim said and then took a breath before continuing.

"Finally, we'd need to do regular cancer screenings plus psychological and developmental assessments to make sure the gene editing we do does not impact your physical or cognitive development. That's it, any questions?" Dr Tim asked.

"How much will this cost us?" Jeff asked.

They both had a number of questions which Dr Tim answered, then he took them to the lab where they would draw blood and took cell samples from Doug in order to conduct his suitability tests.

Before they left Dr Tim had one last thing to say.

"Look, this trial is not for everyone, and it won't change how much you love swimming or the most important things you'll learn from it. This is for people who want to take a chance on getting an extra edge, that's it. Now drive safe heading back up to Muncie," Dr Tim said and then shook their hands.

Afterwards, they went for a late lunch at a barbecue place near the IU Medical Center where Doug at a whole rack of ribs himself. The joy and gusto that Doug ate with always made Jeff smile. Seeing his son's youthful passion for life made him feel a bit younger, even just for a moment.

On the drive back to Muncie, they talked about that morning and how they would explain it all to Joanne. Doug seemed to really want to do it, but then two exits later he would be reticent and wonder if it was a wise thing to do before getting excited about it again. Jeff didn't worry since he knew by now that this was how his son processed things.

"Remember, you have time to think about this since you can't even do it until school is out anyway," Jeff reminded him.

"So, you don't want me to do it?" Doug asked, almost angrily.

"No, I just think it's not something to just jump into." Jeff replied.

"Are you afraid I'll achieve more than you ever did?" Doug asked.

"Slow your roll there, mister," Jeff replied. "When you're young, you measure yourself based on your aspirations. When you get older you measure yourself based on your accomplishments and what kind of person you've become, the lives you've touched, the difference you've made. So no, I'm not afraid of you achieving more than me because I'm living the life I want the way I want, and by my own measures of success" Jeff said. "The question is, what kind of man do you want to be? That is a lot more important than how fast you can swim."

"Sorry Dad, this whole thing is making me crazy," Doug said.

"Look, if you really badly want to do this, we'll find a way. But this is an important life decision," Jeff added.

"Yeah, I could have done this over spring break if I knew all this much earlier," Doug said.

"You'd want to spend spring break in a hospital?" Jeff asked.

"Yeah, good point Dad. Florida is much better."

That night they returned home and explained it all to Joanne who did her best to stay neutral and not be discouraging to her son. Her one response was to flinch when she heard the potential price tag, but Jeff and Doug were so excited, neither one seemed to notice.

Later at bedtime when Jeff closed the door to their bedroom and sat down on the bed, Joanne asked "Are you insane? $56,000?"

Jeff knew this moment was coming so he was prepared to talk about it.

"Look, we only have four more years of payments on the house, and we have more than enough in savings to cover this," Jeff replied.

"Are you counting his college fund?" Joanne asked as she pulled the sheet up to her chin.

"He has a chance to be in the Olympics, wouldn't that make it worth it?" Jeff responded.

"And what if we spend all this money and it hurts him? Or by the time he'd be in college they can test for it, so he's disqualified?" Joanne asked, looking up at Jeff.

Jeff laid back and looked up at the ceiling. He knew she was right.

Sensing she had the upper hand in the argument, Joanne pressed further.

"I mean, spending the equivalent of one year's college expenses on something like this could make it a lot harder to pay for him to go to college if he never gets a scholarship," she added.

"Yeah, it's a big risk." Jeff said. "I just don't want our saying no to be the reason he never realizes his dreams."

Joanne rolled over in his direction and Jeff turned on his pillow, so they faced each other. They lay in the muted light, the remnants of their argument fading like smoke, barely lingering in the air between them. From their pillows, they looked at each other, searching for the familiar comfort they both needed but hadn't asked for.

Jeff's face was lined with the weariness of the day, but there was a warmth in the way his mouth turned, a quiet acknowledgment of the ground they had crossed. Her gaze met his, a flicker of something like apology, or perhaps understanding. They didn't need to speak—the silence was fuller now, filled with the relief of things unsaid.

Their breathing was in sync, an old rhythm they fell back into effortlessly. In the dim light, they were only shapes and shadows, but in this moment, they saw each other more clearly than they had before. Finally, Joanne broke the silence.

"I don't want that either," she said.

"I don't want him to resent us for the rest of his life if we're the reason he never goes to the Olympics" Jeff said.

"Baby, people with great talent train their whole lives and never make it to the Olympics. And they still live amazing and happy lives," Joanne whispered.

"Yeah, but does our son get that?" Jeff asked.

"We can help him understand that" she said softly. "And what if this risky treatment leaves him physically or mentally disabled? Would he ever forgive us? Could we ever forgive ourselves?" Joanne said.

"So, it needs to be his decision," Jeff said.

"Exactly," Joanne replied.

They stayed up later than usual that night to figure out how they could be "supportive but noncommittal" and to keep asking Doug for more information and research which they could all discuss. They figured this would encourage him to learn more and really think about the risks involved and to realize that playing with his DNA may not be worth it.

The next week they all packed up for the drive down to Florida for spring break.

They had left behind the flat, gray winter plains of Indiana, the sky hanging low, heavy with late-winter clouds, and were now, heading south. The light seemed to change, softening with each mile. In the car, there was a stillness, a kind of quiet pact they shared, though no one had spoken much since they'd pulled onto the highway that morning. Joanne and Doug slept most of the first hours so driving duties were left to Jeff who had to keep the music volume down lest they wake up.

The road was familiar, but the silence was not. Joanne slept beside him, legs tucked under her and eyes hidden behind sunglasses though the sun had only just begun to warm the day.

In the backseat, Doug sat sprawled, half-asleep, headphones on, lost in his own world. His limbs long and awkward, still growing into himself. He said little since they left, only a few grunted responses to questions about hunger or comfort.

Somewhere near Lexington, Kentucky they finally started talking about the idea of Doug having his DNA edited, having avoided the topic as long as they could. Joanne asked a number of questions which Doug could not answer, which led him to search for answers on his iPad, blurting them out as he found each one. This always led to additional questions from Jeff and Joanne.

At a certain point, he stopped blurting out answers, having been drawn into reading even deeper into reading what he was finding. Joanne looked over at Jeff and smiled, thinking "our plan must be working."

The hours passed with the steady hum of the tires beneath them mixed with Jeff's 80s and 90s music and the occasional flutter of wind through a cracked window. They stopped at rest areas, gas stations that smelled of coffee and diesel, places where nothing seemed to change. By now Joanne was driving and had switched the playlist to the goth music of her youth. As they crossed into the South, the air grew warmer, the landscape greener. The sky opened up, wide and cloudless, stretching out toward the horizon like the promise of the ocean still too far away.

They would arrive in Fort Meyers Beach by early evening the next day as the sun set after casting a golden light across the water.

The next day, while Doug and Joanne slept late, Jeff had an early breakfast and went to a nearby guitar store to look around and noodle on a used Fender Telecaster they had for sale. He was less interested in buying it than he was in having a guitar in his hands so he would not lose his touch while traveling. He had wanted to bring one along but there simply was no room in the car.

Closer to lunch, they all found their way down to the beach. Jeff and Joanne stretched out on long sun loungers while Doug went off to explore.

The afternoon drifted like the tide, slow and certain, until he found himself among a loose circle of college kids playing volleyball on the beach. The sun cast long shadows, and the air smelled of salt and sweat. Among them was a girl, Celeste, her laugh quick and unguarded, her movements fluid. She was tall and lean, with a ponytail that snapped in the wind, and when it flicked across his face at the net, blinding him for a moment, they both laughed. He missed the block, but something shifted inside him, something small but unmistakable. Her presence, a sudden clarity in the haze of the day, made him forget where he was, what he was supposed to be.

Later, after the game, she stood near him, close enough that he could see the thin sheen of sweat on her forehead. She smiled easily.

"So, what brings you here?" she asked, her voice like the end of a thought.

He hesitated. "Spring break. Needed a break from swimming." The words felt simple, insufficient, but he said them anyway.

She nodded, looking out over the beach, the endless stretch of it. "Same, I guess. Here to have fun. I play volleyball for school, but it's not everything." Her eyes met his, and there was something unspoken between them. "It's easy to get caught up in one thing, isn't it? But life's bigger than just that."

Her words touched something in him, deeper than he expected. Swimming had been everything—his ambition, his escape, his proof to the world. But now, standing here with this girl who moved through life with such ease, his own life felt suddenly narrow, small. There was something about her—this Celeste—that made him want to expand his horizons, even just a little.

Celeste was from one of those quiet, leafy suburbs just outside Chicago, where the streets curve like a whisper and the houses stand with a practiced ease. She was headed for Illinois, to study the past in dusty corners where time collects the buried whispers of forgotten lives. But there was more—she loved horses, ballet, gymnastics. You could see it in the way she moved, graceful without knowing, a kind of elegance that didn't ask to be noticed. On the volleyball court, she was quick and light, like someone who had always known how to fly.

"So, it's like you have your whole life figured out," Doug said.

"Not really, but if my mom taught me one thing it was that balance is as important as any passions we have," Celeste replied.

"Whoa, that is deep," he said.

"It's like this," she began, her voice calm, deliberate. "Without balance, you burn out. You lose yourself in the things you love until they exhaust you, and before you know it, the rest of life feels like it's slipping away. That's when you quit, not because you want to, but because you have to. But if you find balance, you can hold on. You can stretch the passion out, make it last, and somehow, it stays with you longer."

"Ahh, OK," Doug said, now understanding her.

"I've never met anyone like you," he said.

They spent the remainder of the afternoon talking, the kind of conversation that drifted easily, touching on things far from the usual.

By dusk, Doug felt a shift, something subtle but unmistakable, as if the burden he'd carried for so long had begun to loosen its grip.

Joanne and Jeff were stepping out of the water just as they noticed Doug sitting with Celeste, laughter in the air. They exchanged a glance, a quiet joy passing between them—there was Doug, alive in the moment, lighter in a way they hadn't seen in some time.

The next morning they met early, the sand cool beneath their feet, passing the volleyball back and forth in the rising heat. It felt endless, this rhythm, as Celeste, with her easy authority, coached him.

"You'll never make it in doubles if you can't pass," she teased, her laughter bright, as if it could erase the morning haze.

Doug smiled, letting it all wash over him, the way light scatters across water at dusk. Later, they moved through the motions—setting, spiking, serving. Doug, always a moment too late, never quite catching the rhythm, but Celeste didn't mind. She liked the way he moved through things, unhurried, unbothered by failure. There was something easy in him, a grace not seen in boys his age. She had known too many who wore their pride like armor, but not Doug. No, this one had been raised right. She could imagine a mother, calm and kind, who had let him breathe.

By noon, her Uncle Pete appeared, and with him, Gregory—a towering figure, his skin dark and smooth, the way the air feels before a storm, who apparently used to play for the Bahamas national basketball team. Pete had a shock of black hair and an intense focus in his eye that seemed to shoot out past his sunglasses like a laser.

Doug turned to Celeste and whispered "These guys are old; we can take them."

Celeste laughed out loud. "On the beach it's the old guys that kill you. They know how to wear you down since every pass is good and they know how to place every spike or dink."

Doug glanced over, saw Pete and Gregory moving with a fluidity that made the game look easy. Their hands, sure and soft, the ball obeying without question. He felt a sinking in his chest—*oh crap*.

They played Pete and Gregory for a few rounds, both games slipping through their fingers. There were flashes of brilliance—Doug found himself at the net a few times, spiking just enough to steal a side out. But it wasn't enough. Pete and Gregory were machines, cold, calculated, with a rhythm Doug and Celeste couldn't match. They ran them ragged, every corner of the court covered, every angle accounted for. Celeste, impossibly, kept the game alive, diving, digging, retrieving balls that should've been gone. She was everywhere. Every time Doug thought, *that's it*, she was there, pulling off another impossible save.

Doug fumbled in the wake of her efforts, knowing every time she gave him the ball, he was destined to send it into the net or back at Gregory, who waited like a cat ready to pounce. Gregory didn't just hit the ball—he drove it into the sand, as if he was trying to bury it forever.

Celeste never wavered. She played with a kind of quiet joy, smiling through the chaos. Doug watched her, marveling at how little the losses seemed to matter. She was there for the game, for the company, the sunlight. She had a way of being untroubled by the things that seemed to break over him. It was as though she could find joy in the rain just as easily. There was a light in her, one Doug couldn't help but be drawn to.

Jeff and Joanne had noticed. Their son, smitten, unaware of how obvious it was. They let him be, gave him space, knowing the current of things had shifted.

Later, after dinner, Doug walked to the dunes where a party hummed around a bonfire. The sky was vast above them, the smell of salt and smoke in the air. Someone had a speaker, the music drifting from bands like Cannons and The Asteroid No. 4, soft and dreamy, like the night itself.

They sat on the edge of the blanket, close enough to feel the heat but far enough to watch the embers lift and disappear into the air, carried away by the breeze. The fire cracked softly, embers rising like stars.

"Tell me about your swimming," Celeste said, her voice almost lost in the night.

Doug hesitated, then began, speaking in that way people do when they have something to reveal but aren't sure how much to give. He told her about the seasons that had passed, each one leaving a faint trace, and how he wanted to swim in college. His voice grew softer when he spoke of the dreams, the ones that reached toward the Olympic trials, and further still—Los Angeles in 2028, shimmering like a distant, impossible shore. The firelight flickered across his face, his eyes reflecting something both hopeful and uncertain.

"Oh wow, you have big dreams!" she said.

"Aren't they the only kind to have?" Doug asked.

They kissed while the fire tickled them with waves of light and dark across their faces.

"So what is your plan to make all of that happen?" she asked.

Doug paused for a moment, not sure if he should tell her what he was considering but he somehow felt he could trust her.

"Well, other than working my ass off," he said, which made her look at his backside and laugh, "I am thinking about getting my DNA edited to improve my performance."

Celeste recoiled upon hearing these words.

"What?" she said, incredulous. "Why would you do that?"

"I'm not even sure I want to do it but it's on the table," he said. Doug then explained how it all worked, and Celeste asked a lot of questions. The mood of their night had shifted, and he felt her pulling away from him.

"I mean, are the risks even worth it?" she asked. "Is swimming that important to you?"

"I don't know" he said. "It just makes me crazy that the guys I was beating last year are now blowing me away since they had this DNA treatment."

"Oh, so it's your ego then," she asked.

"No.... maybe" he responded. "All I know is that it doesn't feel fair to me."

"So how would it be fair to the others if you do it too? I mean, where does it end?"

"Good point," Doug sighed.

Piling on now, Celeste said "And you don't even know what it would do to you long term. Imagine your life being cut short or someday having kids with birth defects all because you wanted to swim a few seconds faster?"

Doug put his head in his hands and he felt Celeste hugging him now. She no longer felt like she was pulling away from him.

That night, lying in bed, he thought about the gene editing again. Was swimming really worth altering who he was? Was he willing to risk his health, his future, for a few seconds of speed? He thought about his parents, especially his mom, and the way she had looked at him when they discussed the gene editing. She had always encouraged him to be the best, but she also believed in doing things the right way—no shortcuts, no risks that weren't worth taking.

The next night they arranged to have dinner together with their parents. Celeste's mom Lisa was a graceful, classy woman who got along swimmingly with Doug's mom Joanne. Her Dad JP, which stood for Joseph Patrick, seemed to get along with Jeff, even though they had different interests.

JP was nuts about pickleball while Jeff was into the music scene and playing in his band. The one thing they did bond over was college football and whether or not the expanded Big Ten was a good or bad thing.

As they reached the end of their week in Florida, Doug found himself spending less time thinking about swimming and more time reflecting on life outside the pool.

During the long drive back to Indiana, Doug gushed on and on about Celeste while his parents exchanged smirks, smiles, and glances as if to say *is our son in love*?

They didn't even talk about the gene-editing decision until they reached the outskirts of Louisville when Doug told them what Celeste thought about it. Joanne placed her hand on her chest, relieved and grateful that Celeste was talking some sense into her son.

"You have my permission to marry her" Joanne blurted out, causing Jeff to laugh out loud and say, "mine too."

Embarrassed, Doug turned red and said "Aw Mom!"

They all talked through it in over the next few hours and they made one last stop to stretch and fill the gas tank just off I-465 on the east side of Indianapolis. Once they all got back into the car and were fastening their seat belts, Doug took a deep breath and said, "I don't want to do it."

His dad looked surprised. "You sure? This could be your shot."

Doug shook his head. "It's just not worth it, Dad. I want to win because I worked hard, not because I changed something inside me. If I can't be the best the way I am, then maybe I wasn't meant to be. And that's okay. There's more to life than swimming."

His mom turned back to look at him in the back seat giving him a warm, knowing smile. "I'm proud of you," she said softly. Jeff, after a moment, nodded, turning back and placing a hand on Doug's shoulder. "I'm proud of you, too."

Jeff then put the car into drive for the last stretch of their trip home.

By the time they reached the outskirts of Muncie, they had already changed the subject and were talking about what to eat for dinner. Doug also felt a sense of peace he hadn't expected. For the first time in a long while, he wasn't chasing something. He was just Doug, and that was enough.

The next week, Doug called Dr Timothy Joseph to thank him for the opportunity to decline to participate in the DNA trial. His father had offered to call for him, but Doug wanted to do this himself. He wanted to own the decision.

That summer he swam for the Catalina Club and went to visit Celeste three times up in Lincolnshire. He even started to think that maybe he should swim for Illinois. They weren't Florida or Arizona but since his times were good enough, he surely had a chance at a scholarship there.

Closer to Christmas as his senior season was just getting started, he was not seeing any results from his rival Conor Nelson. Was he not swimming this year? He asked Coach Getz about it and a few days later, Doug learned that Conor was experiencing heart problems and had to stop swimming. The other two swimmers were having health problems as well and were being held out of the season as a precaution. Perhaps they could compete again someday but for now, they were done.

# CHAPTER FIVE

# THE SINS OF THE FATHER

*T**he gods visit the sins of the fathers upon the children.*
~Euripides, *Phrixus, fragment 970*

**8pm July 23rd, 2039**
**Chelonos, Greece**

The heat still hung in the air, thick and inescapable, as Maria watched her coffee settle, the steam rising in slow ribbons, warm against her face. She preferred it this way, even now, when the day's warmth hadn't yet faded, and the evening promised little relief. No sugar today, only black as the night falling around her. She sipped slowly, watching as the last traces of sun burned into the horizon, smearing the sky with the final, desperate hues of orange and red before giving in to the encroaching dark.

From the balcony, the sea stretched out, an endless shadow, the shoreline barely visible in the fading light. The Ionian Pearl stood still behind her, its walls absorbing the day's punishment, the heat radiating outward like a pulse that wouldn't stop. But it would, she knew. In a few hours, the cool would come, and the island would wake again. For now, though, it was silent, waiting.

The miners were the only ones who braved the day, returning to their homes and hotels at dusk. The rest had learned long ago—there was no life to be lived under that kind of sun. It kept them inside, hidden away in their rooms, waiting for darkness, waiting for a time they could breathe again. When night came, the island's locals stirred, stepping out into the shadows like ghosts, moving slowly, living in the margins, where the heat couldn't follow. Maria would join them soon. This was her time, the only time that felt real anymore, before the miners returned to The Pearl to end their day, and the locals began their own.

Her mother's voice broke the stillness from inside. "Did the man come? The delivery?"

Maria glanced back into the dim house, its thick walls a defense against the ever-hotter summers.

"Yes, he just came," she replied, turning back to the fading light. "I'll bring it in."

Her mother, small and pale in the glow of a single lamp, sat by a shuttered window, her hands in her lap. Time had worn her down—sun, work, and the slow erosion of age. Her father was in the bedroom, where he spent most of his days now, moving less and less each year. At least he had his books and television.

"I can help," her mother offered, slowly rising.

"No, it's fine," Maria said gently. "Stay where it's cool."

The night was coming on slowly, a soft breeze stirring the air, but the heat still lingered, reluctant to let go. She moved through the hotel lobby, finding the boxes of groceries left behind by the delivery man. Bread, meat, and vegetables wilted by the remnants of the days heat—meager provisions that spoke of the island's slow starvation. Each year the land gave less, the soil cracked and spent, tired like everything else.

She stood there for a moment, listening to the distant hum of the mines, a sound that never quite disappeared, even when the work stopped for the night. Beneath the hills, men burrowed through the earth by day, seeking out the minerals that had become the island's only currency, its last trade after the tourists no longer came. They were digging for something to keep them all going, though even that seemed to be slipping away, just as the land had.

The sea was empty, flat as glass, with only a few boats left upon it. Most of the fishermen had long since given up when the waters warmed, and the fish fled. On land, the fields were no better, sheltered now by a grid of raised solar panels, rows of crops that drank the precious, irrigated water but yielded little in return. the island had once been rich with food and energy, shipping both to the mainland. Now, the food was brought in from elsewhere, and the electricity was consumed just to keep the air cool and lights burning through the endless nights. The island was a place slowly closing in on itself, piece by piece.

Carrying the groceries inside, Maria set them on the counter and floor. Her mother was still gazing down the road, looking as if waiting for something that would never return.

"Do you remember those summer nights here?" her mother asked gently. "The way they used to all be drinking and laughing on the veranda?" Her mother lost in the nostalgia of long-ago nights of revelry, when people would travel from all over the world to witness the island's beauty.

Maria nodded but said nothing. The past hovered over everything now, woven into the fabric of the place like an inheritance that could neither be ignored nor spent.

Later, she had a coffee with her old friend Stavros, as they did most nights. His long legs stretched out before him, a cigarette glowing between his fingers. He was always there, always people-watching. His house, a few blocks away, sagged under the weight of time, passed down to him through generations.

"You're late tonight," he said, his voice rough.

"I was waiting for the sun to set," Maria replied.

He grunted. "Heat's worse today. Feels like it gets worse every year," he began. "You know there used to be more than 100,000 people on the island. Then after the earthquake it took years to even get it back to 35,000," he continued, beginning a script or mantra seemed to have every night.

"Yes, and now we are only 8,000." Maria added. "Over-tourism drove away so many locals that we were almost down to so few when the heat got to be too much."

"First the Germans, then the earthquake, then AirBnB, and now this cruel sun. There is always something trying to kill us," Stavros said, then took a long pull from his cigarette. "So, this is our inheritance, to burn," Stavros finished his oft-repeated complaint as he tapped his cigarette on the ashtray before him.

He noticed Maria was turning her head as if to hear the distant hum of machinery.

"They're finding more down there," Stavros said, nodding toward the hills. "Seems like there's no end to it. Enough to keep them digging for years."

Maria nodded and mumbled "Yeah, if not for them the hotel would be empty and closed."

The miners worked during the day, deep underground, away from the deadly sun. They were outsiders—mostly young men from the mainland, hardened by the work but grateful for the pay. The minerals they extracted—rare metals needed for electric batteries and other new technologies—had given the island a strange, uneasy life-line.

"Your parents were smart to make a deal with the mine instead of waiting for tourists to come back again," Stavros sighed.

"I was living in Germany when they did that. I think they knew there was no other way," Maria said.

"Was that when you were living with Stefan? I never really liked him," he said.

"C'mon, he wasn't so bad. We had many good years together. We just grew apart," she responded. "Still, it left me feeling lost, like I did not belong up there anymore."

"So, you came back home," Stavros said.

"Of course, my parents needed help and I needed a reset. Why didn't you ever try living abroad?" she asked.

Stavros dodged her question and muttered, "Still doesn't feel right," flicking his cigarette into an ashtray. "Digging up the island like that. It's like we're selling our heart."

The island seemed destined to sell its body and soul in order to survive. It was once tourism, now it was mining.

"Can't we make shoes or something else? Anything but this," Stavros motioned toward the mountain across the bay.

Maria glanced at him. He wasn't wrong. The mining opera-tion had saved the island from a complete collapse, but at what cost? The land, already scorched and barren,now had deep scars running through it—tunnels, machinery, and dust clouds that hung over the hills.

"They say Ireland, Scotland, and Scandinavia are better," Stavros said, changing the subject. "Cooler. People still living like normal," he said as he pulled on the skirt of his kaftan.

Maria nodded. She'd heard the same stories about these places where life hadn't been boiled down to a nocturnal existence, where people still lived in daylight. Her cousin Konstantina had written from Ireland, describing green hills and cool evenings, a world that seemed impossibly distant from the heat-ravaged island.

"You ever think about leaving?" Stavros asked suddenly.

Maria didn't answer right away. She had thought about it—leaving the island, going somewhere cool and green, where life wasn't a slow endurance test. But her parents would never leave, and they would never want her to either. They belonged here, in the house they'd always known, tied to an island that was now crumbling beneath them.

"I don't know," she said finally.

Stavros shrugged, his eyes tired. "None of us do."

That night, after Stavros left, Maria stood on the balcony, staring out at the dark horizon. The rumble of the mining machinery had stopped, but the scars on the land remained. The island had been dying slowly, despite the wealth beneath its surface. What was the point of saving it if the land itself couldn't survive?

As the days passed, the question of leaving lingered in Maria's mind. The island, once a paradise, had become a furnace. The few who remained either worked the mines or clung to the edges of life, running shops to serve the miners in the early evening and playing cards under artificial lights. A few people even went swimming at night on a few lighted beaches, but the water was sometimes warmer than the air outside. The minerals kept the economy alive and kept people like

Stavros here, even though there was nothing left of the island they had known.

One evening, as they sat under the olive tree, Stavros turned to her. "You should go," he said softly.

Maria blinked. "What?"

"You should leave. Go to your cousin Konstantina. There's nothing left here."

Maria stared at him, surprised.

But Stavros just nodded toward the hills. "This place... it's dying, even if the mines keep us going for now. You'll regret it if you stay."

The words hung in the air between them. For the first time in years, Maria felt something stir inside her—a spark of possibility. Maybe Stavros was right.Maybe it was time to let go of the island, of the life she'd been holding onto for too long. But she was torn. Who would look after her parents?

Maria woke late the next day. It was almost evening again, the last of the sun's glow casting long shadows across the floor. Her limbs were heavy with sleep, her body reluctant to move. She stretched and sat up slowly, rubbing her eyes as the day died around her.

The heat was still there, lingering, even as the night approached. She pulled on a loose linen kaftan—everyone wore them now, even the men. There wasn't much choice; the heat had made traditional clothing impossible. The idea of tight fabrics,trousers, or anything that clung to the skin, felt absurd and uncomfortable.

The shift had happened gradually, almost without notice. At first, it had been just the women, abandoning trousers in favor of the loose cotton dresses. But then the summers grew even hotter, and soon the men followed. It had been strange at first, seeing them in the same loose garments, moving through the streets like ghostly figures.

Stavros had been one of the last to adopt the change, clinging to his old shirts and pants, but even he had given in eventually. Now, it was rare to see any thing else unless you were working inside one of the mines or it was the coldest part of a winter that didn't really feel like one anymore.

The island had changed, its rhythms, its customs. Everything felt ragged, frayed at the edges. Even gender distinctions had faded. It wasn't something anyone spoke about—it simply was. When the heat became unbearable, some traditions fell away like dead skin, leaving only what was essential.

Maria found it practical, and over time she preferred the aesthetic. They allowed people to move through the long, humid nights with a kind of grace. But sometimes, when she looked at the men, wearing the same flowing fabric, she could sense a discomfort, as though they had lost something of themselves. Their pride, perhaps.

There had been a time when the men on the island held themselves differently. They were fishermen, builders, farmers—broad-shouldered, suntanned, standing tall against the wind and sea. They ruled their villages and families. Now, they walked through town at night in loose dresses, their skin pale from hiding indoors during the day.

One night a few years ago she talked to her mother about this change.

"At first, I didn't like it," her mother said. "The men looked ridiculous and didn't seem like themselves"

"But I've never known a time when people on the island ever felt more equal, Mama" Maria said.

"Yes, it's true and I must say I like that," her mother responded. "The men here were always so entitled, like princes. They expected us to make their beds and wipe their asses."

"And when they got hysterical, it was our responsibility to soothe them and calm them down, as if they were children," Maria added.

"*Nai, kori mou*. But not anymore" her mother smiled as she nodded.

"Is that why *Baba* is so shut down?" Maria asked.

"I don't think so, Maria. Your father loved the bustle of the hotel and the festivals more than anyone so losing all of that dimmed his spirit," she responded.

"He was always a reader but now he is insatiable and reads everything in sight, "Maria observed.

"It's his way to escape into the past, a better time. Everything is better when you're young. And it was better before the world started to boil us," her mother sighed.

Maria was snapped back into the present by her father's voice calling from inside the house, faint and tired. He had barely left his bed in days, his body shrinking into the sheets like a fading memory. She walked back inside and found him sitting up, his eyes dull but awake.

"Is it night yet?" he asked, his voice weak.

"Yes *Baba*," Maria replied. "The sun's gone."

Her father nodded, his eyes drifting back toward the covered window, though he couldn't see anything from where he lay. He had stopped going outside months ago. The heat had taken too much from him, worn him down until all he could do was lie there and read, waiting for the darkness.

"They're digging deeper," he said after a moment, his voice a rasp.

Maria nodded. She knew. They all knew. The mining companies had found a new vein beneath the hills, deeper and more dangerous, but rich enough to keep them digging for years.

"Yes *Baba*, but they are keeping us all alive now," she said. "Without them,there would be nothing."

"They'll dig until there's nothing left," her father muttered, more to himself than to her.

Maria didn't respond. She knew he was right, but there was no point in saying it out loud. They were all clinging to what little remained, trying to hold on to something that was already slipping away.

She left him to rest and went outside again. The courtyard was still, the bare olive trees casting long shadows across the ground. In the distance, she could seethe faint glow of the miners' camp, like a small, distant city. They worked through the night sometimes, though most of them slept during the dark hours,preparing for another day underground.

Stavros was waiting by the Polo Cafe again, as he always was. His hair, once thick and black, had thinned, the long strands tied back loosely at his neck.

"You're early tonight," he said, his voice low.

Maria shrugged, sitting beside him. The stars just beginning to show themselves in the darkening sky.

"Feels cooler," Stavros muttered, though it wasn't much cooler, not really. The heat had become something they lived with, something they carried in their bodies.It was always there.

"They'll be finishing up soon," he said, nodding toward the mining camp. "Big day tomorrow, I hear. They're opening a new tunnel."

Maria glanced toward the camp in the distance across the bay, the distant lights flickering against the hills. She couldn't hear the low hum of the machines since the miners were heading to their homes and hotels now. They would return at dawn, just as the villagers went to bed, their paths crossing only in the briefest moments.

"They say it's dangerous," Stavros continued. "Deeper than any they've dug before. But they don't care, if there's something to take." He sipped on his coffee and looked out on the waters of the bay, shimmering under the moonlight.

Maria didn't say anything at first.

"Yes, we all know the dangers. I mean, who doesn't know someone who got injured down there," she said.

"At least the mines finally brought some decent health care to the island. We never had that back during the tourism boom," Stavros replied.

"And now the nurses and doctors can find houses ever since the tourists went away and took AirBnb with them," Maria added.

"At least there are a few positive things, but I think we're still on borrowed time. The land is too dry and the sea too warm. And some day they'll run out of anything to dig up." Stavros said somberly.

"You ever think about going down there?" Stavros asked after a moment, his voice curious.

Maria glanced at him, surprised. "What?"

"Working in the mines," he said, his eyes fixed on the distant hills. "They're paying good money now."

Maria shook her head. She couldn't imagine it—being underground all day, cut off from the sky, from the sea. The idea made her skin crawl.

"I couldn't," she said quietly. "I need to feel the air, even if it's hot."

Stavros nodded, though his gaze didn't leave the water. "Yeah," he muttered, taking along drag from his cigarette. "Me neither."

"You don't need to worry about money," Maria shook her head at him, smiling. "Your online job gives you more than anything the mines pay."

Stavros shrugged and looked away. They sat in silence for a while, the night settling around them. Maria could hear the faint sound of voices from the square, as the few other residents emerged from their homes as the last of the light disappeared. She imagined them moving through the streets flowing and drifting like shadows under the lit walkways.

They had all adapted, changed, become something different than what they had been. But it still didn't feel real, not entirely.

Just then their friend Burt, an English expat, appeared. Burt had moved to the island 30 years ago during the tourism boom and couldn't bring himself to leave. He kept himself busy fixing up houses and windsurfing at night. Some thought he was crazy, and maybe he was. Maybe that was why he stayed.

"Hey Burt, how are you? Come sit with us!" Maria said.

Burt sat and joined them, and they all ordered a few more coffees.

Maria and Burt talked about music and told a few jokes while Stavros sat brooding. He wasn't angry or put off by the others, but rather he was deep in thought.

After a while, Stavros stood, his movements slow and deliberate. He stretched and swayed in the night air.

"Better get home," he said, plunging his cigarette into an ashtray. "Long night of work ahead with the team in California."

"OK, take care," Maria said.

"Yeah, see you man. Let's play cards soon!" Burt said.

Stavros nodded as if to say yes, then ambled away from the café. They watched him walk back toward his house, like a spirit floating slowly up the hill.

They sat there for a while longer, listening for the sound of a bird. They had not heard one in years but sometimes imagined they had, like a phantom limb that was no longer there. The town was bustling now as it settled into its strange, nocturnal rhythm.

Burt stayed awhile longer then paid his bill and said goodbye, heading over to a hardware store to pick up some things for a house he was working on.

Eventually, Maria left a few euros on the table then walked back to the house just above the Ionian Pearl. The house was now cool and still. Her mother was crocheting in her chair and watching a "morning" talk show on Alpha TV.

Maria went down over to the hotel kitchen where she and their chef Georgia would make meals for the miners who were living at the hotel.

Later,after cleaning up, she stepped out onto the balcony to play her guitar for awhile. After playing a few songs she stood up and felt the weight of the night around her, the faint breeze against her skin. The heat would return in the morning, as it always did, and the miners would go back to their work.

But for now, there was only the night. Only the relatively cool, fleeting moments before the world would feel as if it was burning once again.

The night stretched on, slow and still. Maria wanted to take a nap, but she lay awake in her bed, feeling the air cool against her skin for the first time in days. Sleep hovered just out of reach. She stared at the ceiling, the silence too thick with her thoughts.

She had learned to live in this new cadence, though it often felt strange, as if the island had shifted beneath her, displacing her from what was once certain.She had grown up in this house, born into the rhythms of the island. It was the same house her parents had built, the same hotel that had always been theirs. But now, it felt distant, like a thing borrowed or stolen. The island no longer seemed to belong to her or to them. It was something changed, something unclaimed.

She remembered feeling this way when tourism got out of control in the 2020s, as if selling the island's soul was their only choice. But it was different now. The heat of the 2030s had driven the tourists away, seeking cooler places like Scandinavia, leaving behind a deeper emptiness. This time, it wasn't just the loss of what they had. It was the loss of what could have been—of hope itself, slipping away like the light that had long faded from the sky.

In a few hours, the miners would rise, and she and Georgia would have their breakfast ready, the simple plates laid out as if it were any other morning. The rhythm never changed. They'd eat quickly, in silence or with murmured talk of the work ahead, and then vanish back into the earth, swallowed by the dark tunnels that ran beneath the mountains. By then, the others—those who hid from the sun—would have already retreated to their cool rooms, surrendering to the hours of light that made life impossible. Two worlds, passing in moments so brief they barely touched, like shadows slipping past each other in the narrow spaces of a fading day.

The miners had their dreams, the ones they spoke of at mealtime, plans built on the wealth they believed waited for them in the depths. A house in Sweden, a piece of land in Canada—each of them held to these promises as if they were life rafts, something solid to carry them through the long, unending days. But Maria had seen it before. Nothing lasted. The money, the work, even the dreams—they would all drift away in time, like everything else on this island where no one stayed. Even the miners, she knew, were just passing through, here only as long as the mountains would have them.

Konstantina had written again last week, another message, suggesting she visit. Ireland, she said, was beautiful now. Cool, green, alive with everything that the island used to be. Maria could almost see it—the gentle slopes, the clear air that must feel like a different skin on the face, the soft light falling through the trees in a way she hadn't seen in years. It felt like a place out of reach, a place that belonged to someone else, not to her, bound as she was to this island, this heat, this dust.

But she couldn't quite leave yet. It wasn't even something to consider. Her parents would never go. Her father, his legs giving way more each day, could barely stand. And her mother, still refusing to admit she was fading too, though Maria could see it. She saw it every time she watched her move, slower now, as if the island itself held her, heavy and unrelenting. No, she would stay. It wasn't a choice, it was simply what was.

One early evening, over the clatter of coffee cups and the quiet scrape of bread against plates, Maria broached the subject cautiously, as if testing the air. "I've been thinking about leaving," she said, the words soft but heavy. Her mother, seated across the table, looked up sharply.

"How can you even think of such a thing?" she snapped, her voice rising. "You'd just abandon us here?"

Maria regretted it immediately, the way she always did. "Mama, I'm only thinking about it," she said gently, as if that could soften the blow. "Wouldn't you and *Baba* be happier somewhere cooler?"

Her mother's face darkened with disbelief. "Happier? In a place full of strangers? Are we supposed to make a whole new set of friends at our age?" She shook her head. "I don't have the energy for that. Your father hasn't in years. This is our home, Maria. No matter what."

"Yes, "Maria sighed, "it's your home."

Her mother's eyes narrowed. "And it's not yours?" she pressed. "Ever since you lived in Germany, you came back with all these foreign ideas."

"They're not foreign ideas, Mama," Maria replied, feeling the familiar exhaustion. "I just saw another way to live, that's all. What's so wrong with that?"

"What's wrong," her mother shot back, her voice rising in volume and pitch, "is that now you want to abandon us. You want to leave us here to rot while you go off, make new friends, live some new life while we're stuck here, alone."

"I want a life too," Maria said, her voice tight, trying to contain herself. "I want to find love. I want what you and *Baba* had. Why can't I have that too?"

"We gave you everything!" her mother said, her voice sharp, cutting. "We sacrificed for you. Everything we did, we did for you. And now you're ready to toss us aside, like an old lemon peel."

Maria stared down at the counter, the words sinking in, familiar and bruising. "Oh Mama," she said, her tone turning sharper, "you never answer my question. Why don't you want me to be happy?"

Her mother scoffed, dismissive. "You could have found happiness here, but you're too good for these men now. What about Stavros? He's been your friend forever. Why not him?"

Maria exhaled sharply, her patience fraying. "I've told you a hundred times, Stavros is gay. He's more like a brother to me—sometimes like a sister."

Her mother waved that away, unconcerned. "Well then, what about a miner boy? They make good money, and you'd barely have to see him except on the weekends." She paused, letting the words settle, then added, "Besides, you're not getting any younger. At least you'd finally give us some grandchildren."

The blood rose to Maria's cheeks, her fingers gripping the edge of the sink. She was fuming now, the anger simmering, held just under the surface.

From the bedroom, her father's voice, thick with age and weariness, rose in muffled shouts, the words lost in the walls but the anger clear. It drifted down the hallway, filling the house. Her mother sighed, heavy and sharp, and disappeared into the darkened corridor, her steps fading as she went to calm him. The murmurs continued, brief and low, before her mother's footsteps came back, harder now, her anger gathered like a storm.

"You see what you've done?" she said, her finger sharp, slicing the air between them. "You've broken his heart with this talk of leaving, torn it apart like nothing!"

Maria sat there, her head in her hands, feeling the familiar weight settle over her. No one could weave guilt like her mother, not with that ancient precision, passed down through generations like an heirloom. It seeped into her bones, in every word. Maria didn't reply. She stood, turned, and slipped out of the room, down the stairs, into the waiting night. It was cooler outside, but the heaviness followed her, clinging like the air itself.

A few days had passed, but the silence in the house was a heavy thing, pressing down on everything. Her mother's words still hung in the air, brittle and sharp, while her father had retreated into a silence of his own, not a glance, not a word since that night. The tension was unbearable, and Maria could feel it gnawing at her. She made her decision without much thought, brought him a cold drink, and set it down gently on the table by his bed. The gesture felt small, meaningless almost, but it was something.

He didn't look up. His eyes stayed fixed on the tattered pages of a book he'd read a hundred times, as if the words there were all he had left. She stood there for a moment, waiting for something—a look, a word—but nothing came. It was as though she wasn't there at all. The tears came then, unbidden, spilling over as she turned and left the room, left the house, stepping into the thick air outside like it might somehow lighten the weight in her chest.

She walked until her legs carried her to the old steps that led into Napier Park, where she finally sat and let the sobs come freely. The world blurred around her, the sound of her own crying loud and strange in the quiet of the park. She didn't know how long she sat there—time had a way of stretching in those moments—but eventually, she heard footsteps. Stavros appeared, his familiar shape cutting through the haze of her grief. He saw her and whatever had been on his mind fell away.

Without a word, he sat beside her, pulling her into his arms. The warmth of him, the simplicity of it, broke something loose inside her, and she cried harder, buried in the comfort of his presence. Stavros said nothing, just held her, and for a while, that was enough.

When her tears had slowed, he gently pulled her to her feet, guiding her down the narrow streets, the air cool now as night crept in. They walked to the Polo café, where they sat in the corner, ordered drinks, and waited for the weight to lift. Eventually, Maria found her voice again, quiet at first, but steady enough to speak.

"My father is waiting to die, and my mother is frozen in time. She wants me to stay here and never have my own home or life," Maria said as she shook her head.

"One the one hand, I want to leave and find a place where I can be happy and free, and not live like a vampire" Maria said.

"Don't we all" Stavros chuckled, trying to lighten the mood. "But it's never that simple, is it?"

"Never," Maria replied. "I love my parents, and I don't want to abandon them. I am fucked."

"I know, *agapi'mou*" he said. "But who is looking after you? Why isn't your happiness anyone's priority?"

"I used to really want to have kids and a family but now family just feels like a trap" Maria said. "I don't want children anymore. I wouldn't want to bring them into the world when it's like this."

"My mother wants me to find a miner to marry, can you imagine?" Maria asked.

"So you can see each other for two hours a day?" Stavros asked.

"Yes, she still thinks it's like the old times when men were so dominant that women were happy for them to leave the house," Maria said. "I want a real partner, an equal partner. Someone to love and for them to love me." She sighed.

"And as long as I have known you, there is a river of love in you looking for a sea," Stavros said.

Maria sighed again.

"She pisses me off so much that it makes me want to just leave tonight," Maria said.

"Why not?" Stavros asked. "I mean, I'll miss you terribly but at least you'll have a chance to be happy."

"Why don't you leave?" Maria asked.

"Who me?" Stavros replied. "I've grown to actually like being alone."

"Oh bullshit!" Maria said with a laugh. "I know you hook up with some miner boys, you can't fool me"

"OK, maybe", he said with a wink. "But for me its uncomplicated. Every relationship has an expiration date, so I don't get attached. My heart never gets broken."

"But if you never risk your heart, how will you know real love? The kind that makes you excited to wake up every day?" Maria pleaded.

"I don't think that exists for me" Stavros said.

In the days that followed, the town pulsed with quiet rumors, carried like a hidden current through the streets. The miners had started yet another a new tunnel, more dangerous than the last. The ground was uncertain, they said, prone to shifting, collapsing without warning. But the lure of what lay beneath was too much. The minerals, rare and precious,promised a fortune—enough to sustain the island, to change everything. Or so they said.

Maria walked past the cafés one night, the words drifting to her from the tables where people gathered, their voices too loud,as if trying to shake off the weight of what they knew. They sat in small clusters along the square, their kaftans catching in the faint evening breeze.The old lines, the things that once set them apart, were fading. The heat, the waiting—it had made them all the same.

She saw Stavros at the Polo Cafe, sitting alone,his cigarette glowing faintly in the dark. The smoke rose around him in soft spirals, blurring his face like a memory half-forgotten. He looked older, worn down by something that went deeper than the heat. His skin was pale, stretched thin across his cheekbones, and his eyes—when they met hers—held nothing.

"They say this newer tunnel's dangerous," he muttered, not looking at her.

Maria nodded, sitting beside him. "I heard. So, what are you up to tonight? More remote work?"

Stavros looked annoyed that she was diverting from their regular script.

He tapped the cigarette against the edge of the ashtray, the ash falling soundlessly into the shallow bowl. Then he leaned back, the chair creaking slightly under him, eyes half-lidded as if sleep might overtake him. "It's the only thing keeping us alive," he murmured, his voice low, almost resigned. "But it's killing us too, little by little."

Maria said nothing. There was nothing left to say. Stavros talked endlessly about the mine, the island, the slow erosion of everything they knew. The earth felt brittle beneath their feet, that much was true. She could feel it too, the way the land seemed to crack, its strength bleeding out day by day. But she didn't want to live inside that reality every moment. She wanted, needed, to find something else—some brief, fragile joy. She wished Stavros could, too.

"I've been thinking," Stavros said, his voice low. "Maybe it's time to go."

Maria turned to look at him, surprised. Stavros had never spoken about leaving before. He had always been the one who stayed, the one who held on, even as the others left.

"Where would you go?" she asked.

"Ireland," he said simply. "I've heard it's better up there. Cooler. People still living like they used to."

Maria nodded, her eyes far off, as if tracing the contours of something just out of reach. She'd heard the stories, of course—places like Ireland, Sweden, Denmark. Names that now seemed mythical, where summer still meant something gentler, a warmth that invited rather than burned. People still walked the streets in daylight there, moving beneath a sun that hadn't turned on them. It sounded impossible, almost foolish, the way Konstantina wrote about it, describing a life so different from this one. It was hard to picture now, a world where the sun was a companion instead of a threat.

"You should come," Stavros said, glancing at her. "Get out of here while you still can."

Maria looked across the square. the island pressing in around her like a weight she had carried for too long It wasn't just the heat, though that was part of it, seeping into every corner of her life, into the walls of her house, into her bones. It was everything—the past, her family, the memory of her parents that clung to her like the dust on her skin. She couldn't imagine leaving again, couldn't picture herself anywhere else. Yet the island had begun to feel like a place she was merely passing through, a place where life had stalled.

But part of her wanted to go. The idea had been growing inside her, a small seed of possibility, taking root in the quiet moments when she was alone. She had been holding on for so long, holding on to the comfort of what was familiar, to the island and the people she had known. But what was left for her here? The question had begun to linger like the stifling heat that never seemed to leave. Would she ever find love, or anything like it, on this island that claimed so much of her already?

Stavros didn't push. He sat beside her, his cigarette glowing in the dark. They watched the stars flicker above them, the night stretching on, slow and steady. The air was heavy with everything unsaid, with the decision that hovered between them like a third presence, silent and inevitable, waiting to be acknowledged.

After a long silence Maria stood up, touched Stavros on the shoulder, then walked back toward her family's house. Neither of them raised the subject with each other again for days but something had been churning within Maria.

The mornings were hers alone, a quiet hour that belonged to no one else. Maria would slip from the house before dawn, the air still cool, the world unformed. Her sandals whispered on the narrow path that wound past the marina, now abandoned, and down toward the small stretch of beach beside it. Tetrapolis was still, caught in the last breath of coolness before the day swallowed it whole.

The sea waited, as always, dark and endless. She undressed in silence, letting the cool air touch her skin before stepping into the water. It welcomed her, the chill of it wrapping around her body, pulling away the weight of the days that had piled upon her. She moved further, further still, until the shore became a distant line, a smudge of trees against the sky. Here, floating in the deep, she could forget. She could pretend that nothing had changed, that the island still pulsed with life, with laughter, that she wasn't alone.

When she returned, her skin chilled and alive, her mother was always awake, sitting by the window. But this morning, it washer father. She paused, surprised to see him, surprised that he had risen so early, that he had left the bedroom at all.

"You went swimming again," he said. It was not a question. He knew. Somehow, he had always known. It had been their quiet ritual, her morning swims, her mother waiting, the slow wearing down of time. She hadn't thought he noticed, and yet there he was.

"Yes," Maria replied, pouring herself a cup of coffee. The house was cool now, but soon it would be unbearable again, the heat pressing in from all sides. "The water was nice." She then poured her father a cup of coffee, offering it to him saying "we're all out of milk."

Her father nodded and took the cup, but didn't say anything more. The silence between them wasn't uncomfortable; it was the kind that comes from years of shared understanding.

Maria took her coffee to the balcony railing, staring out at the quiet street below.

Her father quietly sat on a bench behind her.

"I remember when none of those houses were there and we had a clear view all the way to the sea, even from downstairs" her father said, then took a noticeable slurp of coffee.

"It must have been great," Maria said. "So much more space, and the days were nothing to hide from."

"Yes, they were, *kori mou*. But we also had hard times and I was never sure if I should stay or go," he said.

Maria spun around, and said "Really, *Baba*? You almost left?"

"Why do you think I am always reading? It's my escape. It takes me all over the world, away from this burning place," he said.

"*Ela,*" he said as he beckoned her to sit next to him on the bench.

Maria sat next to him, still in shock at what she just heard.

"But why?" she asked. "Why didn't you tell me? Why didn't you talk to me when you knew I was thinking about leaving?"

Her father looked down, as if he could not even look her in the eye.

"It's because I am ashamed. I never had your courage," he said then turned to her. "I'm sorry, Maria. It wasn't fair to you."

She took his hand and said, "I still don't understand, *Baba*."

"Your Uncle Makis had gone to Germany. He wanted me to go with him, and I said I would. But then I delayed, told him I would meet him later," he looked down as his hand moved to his forehead, covering his eyes. "He found work quickly, and found work for me, too," he said.

Maria's eyes opened wide. "Why didn't you go?"

"I was a coward," he said softly, dropping his hand. "I was afraid of learning a new language and culture. I was afraid of failure. I let fear consume me and keep me rooted here," he said.

"Was this before or after you met Mama?" Maria asked.

"It was before I met her and once I fell for her, that was it" he said. "I later tried to convince her to go to Germany with me so I could work with Makis but she wouldn't go. She still had to look after her parents."

"Aha" Maria gently whispered.

"I should have pushed harder to go. We could have even taken her parents with us", he sighed and then took another sip of coffee.

"And because of my cowardice, you did not get the life you deserve. But it's not too late" he said, squeezing her hand. "I think you should go and find your happiness,Maria."

"*Baba*, really?" Maria said, astonished. "Do you really mean that?"

"You are paying for the mistakes I made. It's too late for me, I'm old. But it's not too late for you" he said somberly.

"What about Mama? She is so angry," Maria asked.

"She is angry because I told her you should go," he said. "She understands now. I think deep down maybe she regrets not going to Germany, too."

"Who will take care of you?" Maria asked.

"Oh don't worry about us. I've had arrangements for that just in case, so I am not concerned," her father said.

"I'd still worry about you both," she said.

"What would you do if you stayed here, mind the graves?" her father asked. "You deserve to be happy, to find love, to blossom."

By now Maria was in tears. Her father had not spoken to her this way in many years.

"You can still visit us you know" her father said. "Go find a nice Irish boy and bring him for a visit."

Maria hugged him closely and carefully, since his thin frame felt fragile.

"You carry my hope too. Go and and find love. Go and smile, explore, and live in the daylight again," he said. "If you stay here and rot with us it will break my heart."

Maria's bittersweet tears were in full flow now.

Her mother stepped onto the balcony with the coffee pot and asked if they wanted their cups refilled. She then set it down on a table and sat on the bench on Maria's other side. They all hugged each other closely, crying and laughing.

Her mother then turned to Maria and said, "I think you'd better call Stavros and let him know."

Maria nodded yes through her smiling tears.

They all stayed on the bench together and watched as the sun slowly lit up the sky. And just for a moment, everything was perfect.

# ACKNOWLEDGEMENTS

I am deeply indebted to the many kind friends and colleagues who helped me to shape and complete this book. First off to Geert Cami and the team at Friends of Europe who provided me a platform to write and think about these topics for so many years. I owe a special thanks to my friend and colleague Scott Moreland whom, after reading a short early draft of the story "The Rest of Your Life, encouraged me to "finish the story" and to "keep writing." To my buddy Steve Getz who urged me to write this book and check in on me every few weeks – I can't thank you enough. I'm also grateful to my friends and colleagues Joe Litobarski and Hanna Linderstahl, who both read multiple story drafts and whose encouragement kept me going this past year.

A special thanks to Holly Troy and Megan Minnion, whose inspiration and ideas made this book so much more than it would have been. To my lifelong friend Jeff Decocq, who patiently read every story and gave me pointers along the way, your encouragement and constant support mean the world to me. To Webb Johnson, Mayfan Johnson-Leone, and Michelle Sipes who read the final drafts and gave me excellent feedback, my thanks for your honesty and friendship. To my author friends Stacy Wray and Sarah Martin, thanks for your patience in reading my early efforts and your sage advice that accelerated my progress. To my dear friend Roger Wolsey, your sound advice, support, and encouragement has meant the world to me. And finally to my dear wife Maya Georg, an amazing writer herself. Your undying support, insights, patience, editing, and love made all this possible.

# ABOUT THE AUTHOR

Chris Kremidas-Courtney is a globally recognized futurist and policy influencer who leads efforts to develop collaborative policy approaches to protect and support democracy, equality, and the rule of law in a fast-changing world. This is their first work of fiction.

Made in the USA
Coppell, TX
13 December 2024

42315069R20125